Brooklyn Blitz

Revenge Series Part II

By LaWayne Williams

LaWayne Williams

Copyright

CONTENTS

CHAPTER 1: CHEER UP

"If I'm going to die today, it won't be in these old rags." Four dreary months clung to Aunty Cynthia like a wet bathing suit in a frozen meat locker. Her endless thoughts of Noah were prickly pin needles through her heart. Aunty Cynthia couldn't shake loose the image of her nephew's coffin being lowered into the earth. Her memories kept her on a hamster wheel of visions of Noah's final services.

Aunty Cynthia was the last to leave the burial site. She sat motionless for hours on the lone chair left by the Premier Funeral Home director. The national news reporters had gone to search for their next big story. But low-rate social bloggers lurked in the shadows to capture a photo or video of her grieving. It was an image that would've been easily worth thousands of dollars.

Her stubborn determination outlasted the greediest self-promoting social media reporter. She and darkness were all that remained. The fresh earth seemed inviting. It comforted her aching body as she lay atop the disturbed ground. Her simple, inexpensive black dress was shaded with reddish-brown dirt. Strangely, she didn't shed a tear. Instead, her entire body wept in agony. Medical journals referred to skin weeping by the leaking of affected blisters, but Aunty Cynthia's aging skin was clear from any blemishes.

"Deep breath, I can't let myself be a mess." Aunty Cynthia recited the words that seemed to restore her to a calm state. "Noah is better off with the good Lord and his parents."

Whiiieee. The tea kettle howled loudly throughout the otherwise silent home.

When she opened her eyes from her recurring thoughts of Noah, she was standing in her modest, lived-in kitchen. Aunty Cynthia fasted from any media sources that would remind her of her nephew's death. Noah wasn't just a high-profile slaying, but he was murdered by the same man who had ordered the assassination of a Brooklyn police undercover team. Local and national news markets served up what was birthed the name the Brooklyn Blitz for breakfast, lunch, dinner, and a heavy midnight snack.

"Today is the day I live for me," Aunty Cynthia declared to herself as she stared off into the room with the game pieces still sprawled across the floor. The memory of Noah rummaging in the dark for dice brought what resembled a contorted smile to her face. "This woman deserves to be pampered." As the sole beneficiary of Noah and his father's estate, Aunty Cynthia had millions of dollars to live like an entitled queen. However, she gagged off the idea of becoming a rich snob.

Absent of her surroundings, she soon found herself standing at the bank counter. The teller couldn't conceal his nervous tick. His nose repeatedly twitched. The amount of money in Aunty Cynthia's savings account caught him off guard. He did his best to avoid giving off the impression that he was shocked a meagerly dressed African American woman had so much money. The well-dressed banker covered up his preconceived biases with overt overtures of full-blown ass kissing.

Aunty Cynthia was embarrassed by the attention given to her. She avoided eye contact with the teller and kindly declined the offer of bottled water. The branch manager insisted she should take it for later, but Aunty Cynthia was a homegrown tap water kind of girl and wasn't about to change. She wanted to be treated like any other patron, with only five dollars in her savings account. The unwanted attention was suffocating. Aunty Cynthia rushed away from the bank as if she had a getaway driver waiting for her outside at the curb.

The next hour she spent pampering herself with a Mani-Pedi spa treatment. There were three Vietnamese women in the upscale shop who feverishly worked to please the five entitled American women in the store. Aunty Cynthia was the sixth and refused to show any signs of being agitated about the long wait. When her time came to get her fingernails done, she took a seat and shyly asked the Vietnamese woman to do any style and color she pleased. The nail technician closely spied Aunty Cynthia's facial profile, demeanor, and attire. Her gaze surmised the woman was in her late fifties, with mournful eyes and a motherly appearance.

The technician reached for her brightest red nail enamel. She slammed the bottom of it on the table and, as she grabbed for one of Aunty Cynthia's worn hands, said, "*Bạn phải sống bây giờ*, you must live now." The woman prepped and shaped all ten fingernails before applying the scarlet polish.

Aunty Cynthia would've never chosen such a bright color of nail polish, but sat without complaining. The technician allowed a five second peek for Aunty Cynthia to see her nails before they were gently placed under the curing lamp. Surprisingly, she loved the way her nails made her hands look. As she waited for the timer to sound off, she scanned the salon. The number of impatient patrons had tripled in size.

Too soon! Too many people! Aunty Cynthia thought. She suddenly felt dizzy. She pulled away from the curing machine, hastily stuck her hand in her purse, and pulled out a one-hundred-dollar bill.

In her broken English, the technician said, "Pay over there."

"This is your tip. I gotta get out of here," Aunty Cynthia said without taking a breath.

The technician removed her facemask. Her expression went from surprised to see the amount of the tip to utterly pissed off that Aunty Cynthia had foolishly stuck her newly polished nails into her bag. After checking for any chips in the polish, the petite Vietnamese woman didn't accept no as an answer. Instead, she guided Aunty Cynthia over to the Pedi area.

By the end of the spa treatment, Aunty Cynthia had tipped the technician two crisp hundred-dollar bills. She was thankful for how the caring woman was able to calm her down before she suffered a major panic attack. Aunty Cynthia thought about stopping for something to eat, but thought it best to keep an empty stomach for what she had planned for later in the evening. Raindrops fell heavily from the sky. Aunty Cynthia muttered, "God is weeping for one of his servants."

Her home was a welcoming sight. She completed her day of pampering by taking a thirty-minute hot soaking bath. Afterwards, she put on her best matching undergarments and then the same outfit she wore the night Noah was selected number one at the NFL draft. He had gotten her dress custom made. Thoughts of her nephew and his mother brought a sense of righteousness to her fragile being.

Boom! Boom!

At first she was going to ignore the person beating on her screen door, but curiosity about who it was got the better of her. Aunty Cynthia peered through the peephole and saw a familiar face. It was Darby's father.

"What do you want?" Aunty Cynthia asked without opening her door.

"Cynthia, it's Darby's father, George."

"I know who you are. I asked what do you want." Aunty Cynthia didn't mince words.

"Please let me in. It's raining hard out here. I have a something from Darby," George pleaded.

Reluctantly, Aunty Cynthia opened her door.

"May I come in?" Darby's father spoke with a hurried whispered voice.

"Sure." Aunty Cynthia was ticked off Darby and the rest of her family had been no-shows at Noah's home going. She stepped aside to let George enter.

"Are you alone?" he said guardedly.

"I don't have time for this. You got the wrong one." Aunty Cynthia seemed more like herself. "I don't know what happened to your wife, but I don't have time for games." She glanced over again at the room with the game pieces scattered across the floor.

George's mission was too important to find humor in Aunty Cynthia's response. "No. No. Nothing like that. Farah is in the car. If you don't mind, can she come in too?"

Annoyed she had answered the door, Aunty Cynthia waved her hand in the air to accept another disruption. She sauntered towards her kitchen but stopped mid-stride. Aunty Cynthia tried to walk away to calm her nerves, but she was never known to bite her tongue. Triggered by the sound of her front door slamming, she spun around, prepared to give George and Farah a mouthful of angry bee stinging words.

"Buttercup, please let her go," George pleaded with Rowan, who had run in and quickly grabbed Aunty Cynthia around her legs.

Instinctively, Aunty Cynthia gently put her hands on the little girl's shoulders. "And whose princess is this?"

"It's me, Rowan, Grandma Number Two." Rowan hugged tighter and buried her head alongside Aunty Cynthia's hip.

"Rowan, let her breathe," Farah spoke in a non-punitive tone. "We talked about taking it easy."

"Yes, Grandma." Rowan relaxed her hold and slowly backed away from Aunty Cynthia.

The two of them stared at each other. Rowan waited for Aunty Cynthia to say it was okay that she could hug her again, but Aunty Cynthia couldn't find her own voice. Rowan's resemblance to her nephew was unmistakable. Aunty Cynthia didn't need Farah or George to confirm what her eyes had already deduced; the little girl they brought to her house was Noah's child.

"But why now?" Aunty Cynthia's thoughts ran wild. "This girl must be at least five or six. Did Noah know? He had no clue cause if he did, he would've said something to me." Her annoyance began to boil over. "Damn them!"

"Grandma Number Two, you have such a pretty dress," Rowan said gleefully.

Aunty Cynthia fell to the floor and bawled her eyes out like a mourning mother. A pill bottle she had held hidden in her hand showed itself for the first time. It rolled on the floor before stopping at Rowan's little red sneakers. Farah and George stood speechless.

CHAPTER 2: REPLAY

Whisper listened to the voices of his daughter and ex-wife tell morning razzing stories that at times brought joyful laughter and tear-filled eyes. Their merriment was just the right dose of medicine he needed to complete his next mission. He stayed camped outside of their home. He hid within the thicket cover of the trees and bushes that surrounded the dwelling where he once resided.

He had foolishly thought being free from doing Chameleon's bidding would've given him a sense of piece, but he had never been more at unrest than ever before. Whisper had been hiding in the same bushes for more than two weeks. He was hoping no one would harm the only two people he'd allowed himself to love. He had prepared enough rations to camp out for several months or until his killer instincts led him to believe no one was sent to murder his only resemblance to family.

In between the lapses of still voices, Whisper occupied his time by reminiscing about the days when the three of them were a semi-happily functioning unit. His illegal and extremely dangerous occupation of being a hired gunman never set well with Terry, his ex-wife, but the circumstances of how they met afforded her blind-eyed acceptance.

By the age of sixteen, Terry had been working two jobs that only paid her cash. During the day, she had established a steady client-based dog-walking gig and at night worked as a bartender at her uncle's pub and grill. She had always looked more mature for her age, so she mostly dated guys who were older than her. She had unwittingly attracted the attention of an older boy who treated high school as a social gathering place.

Dylan, the leech of a boyfriend, had attached himself to her almost the first day Terry entered high school as an aspiring freshman. For two years, he had managed to hide his ever-increasing drug dependency from only Terry. Except for her, he was a large walking roadside billboard to why it was important to just say no to drugs. He started with a hard case of recreational marijuana, but quickly began to con and steal to feed his insatiable appetite for heroin and oxy.

Her closest friends, parents, and teachers who cared for her wellbeing tried to get her to see the human mistake that walked alongside her with his arm always wrapped around her shoulders. But she loved him like someone from PETA who was nursing a severely abused puppy back to good health.

It was on her eighteenth birthday when Terry was forced to declare emancipation from her justifiably concerned, protective parents. They had grown too weary of the Terry and Dylan saga. Her parents presented her with an overgrown steroid looking cupcake with strawberry icing and a single lit candle erected from the center of it.

"I hope you wish for the vision to see the wickedness in him and the strength to leave his sorry ass," her mother said. Then she blew out the candle for Terry. "I'm sorry, but he's not good for you!"

Embarrassed by her mother's insensitive outburst, Terry looked over at Dylan. "Yes, I'll move in with you." It was a question she had been wrestling with until that very moment.

After just two months of sharing a meager one-bedroom apartment together, Terry was the sole bearer of maintaining rent, household essentials, and their groceries. She picked up extra hours at her uncle's pub and decided to put college on hold for a year. Dylan enjoyed his freedom from the daily hustle of life by escaping reality by popping pills, sniffing, or shooting up more and more drugs. Eventually, Dylan pissed off the wrong bad guy by borrowing away his last lifeline. Repayment was no longer an option, so with a simple gesture of a slight nod of his head, a younger Whisper was given the order to take out Dylan and make it messy, too.

Whisper had over twenty kills under his current employer, so he knew just how messy to make the hit. It wasn't difficult to track down Dylan. Terry's boyfriend left obvious traces of himself wherever he had gone. For a guy who was in debt to a really bad guy, Dylan went about his business like usual—reckless.

The hit was to take place at their apartment. Whisper would kill anyone who had the misfortune to be in the home that night. He wanted Dylan to watch his loved ones die before his pathetic eyes. Dylan's fate wouldn't be quick. Whisper planned to torture him throughout the night. He was prepared to only stop once he wasn't amused anymore.

Tap. Tap.

Whisper rapped on the door with his fully loaded Rugger 9mm. Dylan swung the door open without a care for who was on the other side.

"Come in. I've been expecting you for a while now." Dylan turned his back on Whisper and headed to the lone bedroom where Terry had been resting from her double shifts of work. "T, get up. I need you to do me this solid."

Dylan shook Terry hard enough that she awoke instantly.

"AAAAHH!" Terry screamed at the sight of Whisper and the gun he was wielding around the room.

"Look at her. She's gotta be worth five times what I owe." Dylan caressed Terry's face as he spoke. "T, I need you right now."

Terry was too frightened to speak.

"T, just do this for me one time. Then we can have that damn baby you've been wanting." Dylan tugged and clawed at her pajama top, which was the only piece of clothing she was wearing. When she resisted, he tore open her shirt. Buttons separated from the thread that held them in place.

"STOP!" Terry screamed in utter shock. "What are you doing?" She tried her best to conceal her exposed body, but Dylan continued to rip at her arms and hands.

Shoop!

Dylan's hands and body went motionless. Whisper could now see straight through the new hole he'd created in Dylan's head. Disgusted by what he'd seen, he'd put the muzzle of his 9mm to Dylan's head and pulled the trigger.

"I chose him over my family." Instead of being terrified at having her boyfriend's blood and brain matter splattered all over her, Terry only felt foolish for believing in Dylan. "I was stupid enough to think I could help him." She took her attention off her pathetic but very dead boyfriend and looked at Whisper. "I hurt my parents. I can't go back." Her eyes indicated she was at peace with her immediate fate. She welcomed the idea of death.

Whisper hadn't worn anything to hide his identity. Terry had seen his face and he could see she wanted him to end her life. She was a liability that needed to be dwelt with before she jeopardized his employer's illegal operation. He could put a bullet in her head right then or wait to be ordered by his employer to do it later in the shadows of the night. In either case, he knew what he had to do.

"Come with me."

These three simple words meant that if she chose to go with him, he'd protect her from any harm.

CHAPTER 3: YOU GOT THIS

George didn't wait to be given permission. He said, "Farah, take Rowan into the next room."

"Don't you freaking judge me!" Aunty Cynthia spoke angrily. "Noah was all I had left!"

George said, "I'm not here to judge you. Not in the least. We are here to seek your help in properly raising Rowan. My daughter wants her to know both sides of her family."

"Oh, is that a fact?" Aunty Cynthia said sarcastically. "Then why didn't Darby bring Rowan to her father's home going service?"

George fidgeted with his sterling silver *Best Dad* bracelet as he tried to search for the right words to say. The noise from his fingers rubbing across the band transmitted a shuffling sound back to Darby. She was about a half-mile away, listening to her dad stumble over his words to try to make things right. Darby knew it should've been her to tell Aunty Cynthia about Rowan, but with everything that happened, it wasn't safe for anyone to know her whereabouts.

Darby had kept her distance since taking a direct shotgun blast to the chest. Her tactical bulletproof vest level III had done its job of preventing any fatal injuries, but she'd suffered some cuts to her head and arms after the force from impact projected her out the large glass plated window. She acted purely on adrenaline and fear of never seeing Rowan again to quickly muster up the strength to get up and take cover in a nearby backyard.

Oddly enough, it was Agent Barr, her obsessed partner, who tracked her down that morning before anyone saw the unconscious FBI agent with bloody hair. When Darby had failed to report in at a scheduled time, he barely waited for the next three-hour checkpoint undercover agents were given before initiating the full out search party.

"My nephew would've been there for her. He loved her, but it's obvious your daughter travels on one kind of road—one way." Aunty Cynthia was just ramping up about her distaste for George's absent daughter.

Darby felt as if she had intentionally placed her exposed hand in a violently active beehive. Aunty Cynthia's words stung hard to her core. "I should be the one telling her how much I loved Noah and still do!"

She put her face in her hands. Then she stepped on the brake and pushed in the ignition button. Darby's rental came to life. She shifted the gears into drive and lifted her foot off the brake. The mid-sized SUV's tires didn't make a full rotation before Darby smashed down on the brake pedal.

"I have to keep them safe." She tried convincing herself that she was staying away to keep Rowan, her parents, and Aunty Cynthia safe from harm, but that was only partially the reason. Truthfully, she couldn't imagine how she could tell Aunty Cynthia that her nephew Tyrus was still alive, but she wouldn't rest until she killed him for murdering his brother, Noah.

"Dad, you got this. Convince Aunty Cynthia she needs to live on for Rowan's sake." Darby said aloud in her car.

Fortunately for Darby and her father, unexpected kid innocence saved the day. Rowan had broken free from the attention of her grandmother, Farah. She ran into the room where George and Aunty Cynthia were having a heavy, one-sided seesaw conversation where Aunty Cynthia had her feet firmly planted on the ground.

"Grandma Number Two, let's play a game." Rowan grabbed Aunty Cynthia by the forearm and lightly pulled her in to the direction of the room with the fallen game pieces.

Aunty Cynthia hadn't visited that room since the death of Noah. If she were the therapist type, she would've been advised to straighten the room up so she could begin the healing process. But Aunty Cynthia was far from someone who believed in telling strangers any of her business, and she gave advice much more than ever accepting it. Yet being guided by the hand of a small child would be the start of Aunty Cynthia's Road to recovery.

CHAPTER 4: HEALING PROCESS

Tyrus was still healing from his expensive plastic surgery. His facelift had gone better than expected and he hardly felt the post-surgery pain. "Nothing but the best doctors for me," Tyrus gloated. "Chameleon, you thought you could outsmart me. Yup, see where that got you—dead."

He basked in the fact he had beaten his nemesis by taking his money, life, a few illegal connects, and his number one hit man, Whisper. Tyrus was experiencing a runner's high over how his plan not only destroyed Chameleon but also took out his know-it-all brother Noah. He'd have the ultimate high if Aunty Cynthia would off herself in the coming days.

Tyrus had watched Noah's funeral proceedings by way of a secured miniature camera attached to Big 60's gaudy Texas belt buckle, ready to finish off Darby if she had showed. Tyrus had paid special attention to Aunty Cynthia. He watched her as she sat with a blank look on her face as lousy mourners came from all directions to offer their useless condolences.

"Aunty, it was me! I killed your wonder boy. Me! That's who!" Tyrus had said with anger in his voice as he watched.

The mask he was wearing on his face shifted. He adjusted it so it rested comfortably back on his face. Except for Big 60 and the plastic surgeon who didn't know his usefulness was coming to an end, there were no others who spoke to Tyrus without seeing a mask on his face.

Tyrus and Big 60 hatched a scheme that the face of the organization would become Big 60 with Tyrus behind the controls. They didn't want to leave anything to chance, especially since Darby could still be alive. She was a problem that needed to be erased forever.

To avoid the heat that was coming from the aftermath of the Brooklyn Blitz, Tyrus setup shop in south Jersey. He didn't want to stray too far from New York, where he was most comfortable with his newly acquired gun contacts.

The movie *Scarface* was on repeat in his sprawling living room. Tyrus idealized Al Pacino's character, Tony Montana. "I have to be smart and ruthless without second guessing my decisions." Tyrus was well aware of how the movie ended, but would have it no other way than to go out with his own gun empty of rounds.

"Today."

Tyrus texted Big 60 the code word to activate Whisper.

CHAPTER 5: PSYCHOLOGIST

The Brooklyn Blitz wasn't just a simple gun-blazing shoot out for a rookie detective to experience; it was a massacre. Consequently, Detective Kate Lawson was a coil that had been stretched too loosely and possibly wouldn't ever return to her original self.

Detective Lawson was ordered to take a few weeks off and be cleared by the department's psychologist before returning to work. She managed to overcome a perceptual collapse by channeling an absurd amount of focus on the status of the sniper. She had read over Detective Ross's witness statements for the umpteenth time and, without fail, would agonize nightly if the sniper was still alive.

"Did he get caught in the crossfire or was the cop killer alive and smirking at what he did?" Her thoughts of the sniper never left its own hamster wheel. "I owe it to my fallen brothers in the force, especially Detective Nine. I promised her I would make the arrest or make him pay with his life."

The morning after the Brooklyn Blitz, Detective Lawson suffered an anxiety attack that only tossing and breaking objects in her meager apartment helped her overcome. Then she was emotionally attacked by survivor's remorse. Detective Lawson comforted that impulse by shaving her hair off like Demi Moore in *G.I. Jane*. Except for being well endowed, her resemblance to the star actress was uncanny.

Mesmerized by her light green eyes, top model physique, and too pretty to be a cop face, her psychologist ignored the telltale signs of someone who was trauma stricken and beyond her breaking point. Instead, he allowed his teenage boy-like crush and lustful thoughts to rule that she was fit again for duty.

By the end of her sessions, she had added muscle mass to her already toned body, sported a tomboy hairstyle, and ditched her conservative clothes for form fitting jeans and tops. Detective Lawson was badass personified. Her reality of life and fear of death no longer affected her way of living.

With the signed released papers scanned to headquarters, Detective Lawson finally reacted to one of the countless sexual advances made by her handsy psychologist. She pinned him to the wall behind his desk with her body. Although caught off-guard, he didn't resist. Their force knocked over a five by seven inch desk picture frame of his pudgy wife and three kids. He paid no attention to the noise of it crashing to the floor.

"You want me." Detective Lawson stroked his jellylike arms. "I sprayed my hair with a sweet scent just for you."

Standing about a foot taller than her, the aroused psychologist bent his head forward and leaned down a bit to take in a deep sniff of her short hair.

Like a shotgun recoil, Detective Lawson jerked his arms down to his sides while simultaneously ramming her head into his exposed nose.

"You broke my nose!" he said in a muffled voice. Blood ran into his mouth. "Ooh!" He tried to stop the bleeding by pinching his nose, but the perfectly placed knee to his groin sent him squealing to the floor. Instinctively, he grabbed at his crouch.

Detective Lawson left him squirming on his office floor next to the shard pieces of glass from the broken family photo frame.

CHAPTER 6: TRASH

Detective Lawson returned to duty without showing signs of wear. Lt. Tiana Marks, her supervisor, was happy to have her media created action hero and on and off girlfriend back in the fight against injustice. They had managed to keep their relationship on the hush from everyone on the force except for the late Detective Nine.

"Kate, welcome back. Come to my office in five," Lt. Marks directed.

On her first day back, Kate wanted to avoid emotionally draining topics and people. Lt. Marks was on top of that very short list to be dodged at all costs. "Ma'am, can we talk later? I want to—"

"Ma'am? Really? It's LIEUTENANT if you want to be formal. Now you have four minutes." An agitated Lt. Marks stormed off to her office.

The new badass Kate was still no match for the formidable Lt. Marks. She walked closely behind Tiana with her back hunched over. The glass office showed an attractive African American woman pacing back and forth. But worse, it looked as if she was talking to herself. Kate took in a deep breath before knocking on the frame of the door.

"Come in and close the door." Lt. Marks continued to pace in front of her desk.

Kate wanted to take a seat but since she had made it formal, Detective Kate Lawson knew she needed Lt. Marks to extend her the courtesy.

"Did I miss a memo?" Tiana scratched at her short Halle Berry pixie cut styled hair.

"What?" Kate was clueless.

"You know. The memo that said we were broken up." Tiana's eyes watered, but the tone of her voice meant business. "I called you. Stopped by your place and waited outside but you ignored me. It's like you threw us away with the trash."

Kate was angry with herself because she didn't feel any empathy for Tiana. To keep from falling apart, she needed to focus on the sniper. However, Kate knew she needed Tiana as an ally, especially if she wanted to stay close to the Brooklyn Blitz case files. So, she chose her words carefully.

"Tia, I'm sorry. I just needed time to myself." Ignoring who could see in the office, Kate grabbed Tiana's hand. "I never meant to hurt you."

Tiana accepted Kate's touch of her hand and didn't pull away. She needed her girlfriend back and didn't care who saw. "Are we still a thing?"

Kate wanted to say no to spare her love the heartache that would possibly come later, but again needed the resources Tiana could give her. "Of course we are. If you still want us."

Tiana gave Kate a sincere hug and whispered in her ear, "I will never let you go."

At that moment, Kate glanced down at Tiana's desk. There was an old photo of the late Detective LaQueesha Nine and Tiana together. LaQueesha, being ten years older, was pushing three-year-old Tiana in a stroller. They were first cousins and one of the main reasons Kate wanted to dissolve her relationship with Tiana. Kate struggled with knowing her lover's cousin had sacrificed her life when it was determined and confirmed by the disgraced Detective Ross that the objective was to capture Detective Nine, not kill her.

"Okay." Kate tried pulling away, but Tiana didn't loosen her grip.

Helpless to her exasperated feelings for the woman she so deeply loved, Tiana whispered, "See you tonight."

To Kate, those three words were worse than if Tiana had said she loved her. She felt trapped—say no and lose any chance of getting information from the Brooklyn Blitz, or say yes for a night filled with an emotional hurricane of feelings.

"Yeah. Sure. Talk more tonight," Kate finally responded.

Kate spent the rest of her duty shift with anxious nerves. Her encounter with Tiana gave her the same scared sensation she had when she hid behind the dumpster as Detective Nine stood her ground for the last time.

"I should've died that day a hero not still living as a coward." Kate sat at her desk with self-hatred. "I'm not ready. Too soon." Beads of sweat formed on her forehead. She started doing her breathing exercises to regain her composure. "Smell the flowers. Blow out the candles." She repeated that cadence four more times before her heart rate settled to a normal rest state.

At times, it appeared the hours were a stubborn child refusing to move forward. Kate tried to find something that would keep her occupied but on her first day back everyone treated her as if she had *Handle with Care* stamped in red across her forehead. Lt. Marks tied the bow on Kate's miserable day by the countless unnecessary visits to the detective unit and her overt passersby touches on various parts of Kate's upper body.

Detective Lawson's shift finally ended at five-thirty in the early evening. She wasted no time getting to her recently purchased Firecracker Red Wrangler Unlimited Sport Altitude 4X4. To Kate it was Double-B, Bold and Badass. Her self-assurance grew and grew the closer she got to her jeep. Once she was inside and the engine roared to life, her confidence was as fearless as a gamma infected She Hulk.

"You can do this," Kate spoke loudly to her ego. "Don't let anyone get in your way, including Lt. Marks." It felt easier for Kate to refer to Tia as Lt. Marks instead of the pet name she used for her lover.

At home, Kate quickly kicked off her black heels, shimmied out of her formfitting jeans, and tossed her burgundy crisscross blouse onto the bed. She froze in front of her full-length mirror that hung on the closet door. Kate shivered a bit as she remembered how it felt to be touched by Lt. Marks. She escaped from those unwanted feelings by going for a quick 5K run.

"Hi babe." Lt. Marks was waiting on Kate's steps. "I called you, but I see why you didn't answer. We could've gone together."

Kate was an avid runner, but Tia had run cross-country in high school and at the collegiate level. She would run whenever Kate invited her to do so, but hung up her passion for running to take on the desire to move quickly up the ranks in the NYPD. It was still light out for Kate to see that Tia was wearing her favorite go-to one-piece military tank dress. It accentuated her athletic curves, abs to die for, and perky in-your-face blessings.

"Yeah. I left my phone in my apartment." Kate liked to hear the sounds of the city as she ran. She paused for a moment as she readied herself to unlock the outer door. "Come in." Kate closed the door behind Tia and went to fasten the lock. "Uhh ..."

Tia pushed Kate's face first against the door. It was so quick that Kate didn't have time to be startled. Tia pressed her body against

Kate and touched her left ear with her lips as she whispered, "I missed you."

"I'm sweaty. Not like this." Kate peppered Tia with excuses. "I just finished running."

Tia spun Kate around without giving up ground. They faced each other. Tia had a slight height advantage, but both stood eye leveled. Tia nibbled on Kate's lips and gently pecked at her neck. Tia removed Kate's waistband that concealed a small handgun and started tugging at the edges of her leggings.

"This is really happening," Kate thought as she watched her bellyband fly through the air and land quietly on her loveseat. She felt fortunate the leggings she wore had a drawstring that she tied tightly before her run. "Tia, I'm sweaty."

Tia slowly pulled her head back to spy directly into Kate's eyes. "I love you."

Kate was cockily proud of the fact she was still able to keep her feelings checked, while Tia's were at full throttle. Kate knew this was the time for some pillow talk. Until that moment, she had kept her hands to her side, but began rubbing Tia's hips. She watched as Tia's eyes closed as her body welcomed the familiar sensations of her lover's hands.

"I love you, but if we are going to work, I don't want to be treated like a helpless survivor." Kate deliberately paused and ran her fingers through Tia's short hair.

"I won't," Tia said with a heavy breath. "I promise." Her eyes never opened but her hands saw to finally unfastening the drawstring that kept Kate's leggings from falling.

Kate knew it was time to bind Tia to her promise. "I want you but a shower first."

Tia opened her eyes and softly kissed Kate on the lips. She smiled as she confidently let her dress fall to the floor, revealing nothing but her beautiful ebony body. "I'm about to put my spell on you." Tia walked with a seductive confidence towards the bedroom.

"You just knew you were going to get some tonight," Kate said, as she took off her sports bra.

"Who can say no to this?" Tia said as she motioned with her finger for Kate to follow her.

CHAPTER 7: BAIT

Big 60 texted, "*Irritating fly.*"

The message was quickly received on Whisper's burner phone. "These two are such a joke, but I can't turn away a fifteen percent pay increase," Whisper thought. "When the money dries up, I'll leave or put them both to sleep for good."

The words irritating fly were the go ahead to take out the now disgraceful whistleblower Detective Ross. He was the one who had connected all the dots for the DA's office. Chameleon's empire and informants had gone crashing down as a result. Many were arrested or killed trying to escape police custody. The few fortunate ones went into hiding before their doors were kicked in.

Whisper briefly left the comfort of his surveillance in the bushes for a vacant apartment high-rise. He prepared his semi-automatic Barrett M82 for the mission at hand. It was definitely more than what was needed, but besides making a huge statement, he wanted something with enough punch to penetrate the body armor he expected Detective Ross to be wearing. Whisper assembled the rifle from muscle memory while his mind was still focused on what could be happening at his ex-wife's home.

He had commandeered a single room apartment that had a good vantage point to the small police courtyard that led to the transport area. Whisper knew he would only have about thirty seconds for Detective Ross to walk from the building to the armored vehicle. The time span would shrink considerably with the number of officers who shielded the disgraced detective.

Detective Ross finally walked out wearing a fully shielded Kevlar helmet.

"Go big or go home," Whisper thought. He was glad he had chosen the Barrett M82.

The bulletproof body suit they had dressed Detective Ross in looked like it was custom made for his meager build. Surprisingly, there was only a four-person escort team. They protected his north, south, east, and west. Whisper recognized Kate Lawson, the female detective from the Brooklyn Blitz. She was covering Detective Ross's backside.

The officer who had been leading the escort team to the bullet resistant van stopped momentarily to accept defeat from his seasonal allergies. His body heaved as he sneezed into his elbow. The pause was all Whisper needed as he anticipated the next time Detective Ross would turn his head in the direction of the street.

"I determine who lives or dies. Today, you die." Whisper squeezed the trigger. The bullet sped from the gun with an eagerness to hit its target.

The bullet drilled through the shield straight into the target's brain. Detective Ross slumped to the ground. Three of the officers went into a tactical defense mode as they tried to drag his lifeless body back towards the building.

CHAPTER 8: GAME ON

Whisper had made quick work of the disgraced Detective Ross. He gasped for one breath before closing his eyes forever. His body was hard to maneuver, but two of the four-man team attempted to drag Detective Ross's body back towards the building, while one provided cover.

Kate's attention was fully committed to the sky and the possible building the shooter had used to kill the city's biggest informant they'd had in decades. She had a hunch that the Brooklyn Blitz sniper was still out there killing people, but needed confirmation. Although she kept the team small to minimize the potential numbers of fatal casualties, Kate was willing to sacrifice her team, as well as her own life, to satisfy her suspicions.

She was not a gambler, but she rolled the dice on the fact the sniper was a professional whose sole focus was to take out those on his contract kill list. Kate had not intended to let Detective Ross rot away in prison. She had told anyone who cared to listen or in earshot what day her team would transport Detective Ross, hoping word would get back to the sniper.

Whisper spied through the scope of his gun to observe the body language of Detective Lawson. A sinister smiled creased through his usually serious face as he tilted his head slightly forward as a gesture of thanks. Whisper realized he was just in a game of cat and mouse. A game he was too eager to play with the lady detective.

Instead of concealing his location, Whisper stood tall as he dissembled his rifle suppressor with intentional sloth like movements. He was sure that the naïve detective would eventually see his foreboding silhouette.

"Ha-ha." Whisper couldn't contain his laughter as he thought of a mouse daring to chase a ferocious cat, especially one like him, who had lion-like instincts.

"You pompous ass," Kate said through clenched teeth. At the height and distance away, she couldn't make out his face, but it was unmistakable he was holding a rifle. "Game on."

CHAPTER 9: SHOELACE of TROUBLE

Darby was still savoring the fact Rowan had finally met someone from Noah's family. The thought of her daughter growing up and hearing how great a man her father was to his family, friends, teammates, fans, and community was worth her doing everything in her power to preserve his legacy.

She sat in her car and watched two people sitting inside a Manhattan diner eating a late lunch. The man she was familiar with, but she knew very little of the woman that kept him company. Darby had a great vantage point of the window booth seat they occupied. She had been keeping a tight leash on them since Noah's home going. In between her solo recon of the people responsible for Noah's murder, she managed to keep track of their comings and goings.

There were several times Darby wanted to reveal herself to Liam, Noah's childhood best friend, but secretly wished he would leave New York. However, with critical Intel in hand, the time had finally come to bring on allies to assist in her scheme to exact revenge on those that did not deserve to live.

Liam O'Carroll, the recently crowned UFC heavyweight known by fans and foes as Hurt, sat uncomfortably cool. His bulk seemed to dwarf the size of the booth. Darby's quick Google search revealed the woman was Indigo, his primary trainer and corner woman. She appeared to be solely focused on every word uttered by her massive trainee. Her slim but muscular, toned body shook with exaggerated movements. It was obvious to Darby that Indigo had strong feelings for Liam that went beyond trainer and friend, but he sat with the emotions of a rock.

While the two of them ate casually in the restaurant, Darby sat in her car watching her surroundings. She had spotted a young teenage couple that had to be seniors at the local high school. A newly affixed bumper sticker on their car read: Senior's Rule the World. The male driver circled twice before finding a manageable New York City spot to park. He struggled to parallel park, even with the use of a rear car camera. He was seen shushing his companion as her hands flailed in many directions to keep up with the rapid pace of her mouth.

She heard the female passenger yelling, "Turn the wheel. Stop. Put it in reverse. I think you hit that car!"

After giving slightly hard taps to the bumpers to the cars in front and behind him, the male driver finally managed to get most of his car in the parking spot. The alarm of the car in front of him sounded off, so everyone knew something was wrong. However, inside the young couple's car, the female's cheers for her man's accomplishment drowned out the ringing noise. A proud smile shone on his innocent face. His sweetheart raised her arms in a victory formation. The two of them giggled with laughter.

Darby was reminded of her fun college years spent with Noah, the love of her life. She was Noah's number one fan and head cheerleader for the great things he did on and off the football field.

Attempting to be a gentleman, the senior unbuckled his seatbelt, rushed out of his driver's side door, and walked around the back of his car. He stopped momentarily to fasten his loose shoelace, but still managed to open his sweetheart's door before she tried to exit the vehicle.

"Where the hell did you go?" Her agitation seemed to take him by surprise.

"What? I just walked around the car to open your door. You should be thankful," said the unapologetic male driver.

With her head and hands moving in offended unison, she argued, "What insignificant … want-a-be-me … did you text?"

"Girl, you trippin'," he said.

"Well, I just picked myself up and woke up. Take me home!" she demanded.

"I thought we were gonna to eat." He shrugged his shoulders in disbelief.

"Apparently, your menu of choice is filled with rotten fish." She mugged him in his face.

Darby couldn't contain her laughter. It was Noah and her all over again. She'd accused him on many occasions of sleeping around with his star struck groupies but had never found evidence of it. Darby couldn't live with the fact that one day he would, so she concealed her pregnancy with their baby. She left Noah before he could hurt her. An unforeseen storm of emotions overwhelmed her spirit, causing her laughter to take a back seat to a minute of sorrowful thoughts.

LaWayne Williams

Beeeeeep! Beeeeeep!

The male driver angrily bullied his way out of the parking spot with no regard for the damage he caused to the other cars.

CHAPTER 10: ALLIES

About an hour later, Indigo and Liam exited the restaurant. Their waitress was seen jumping with excitement about the hefty one-hundred-and-fifty-dollar tip Liam had graciously left for a thirty-five-dollar meal.

He now earned a substantial amount and had a lot of fame thanks to the UFC, but it was the five-million-dollar estate his father had left his only child that had Liam wanting for nothing. Liam didn't look or act the part of a rich, snobby beneficiary. Instead, he purposefully refused to lean on his father's good fortune. To him, it was money that needed to go to a worthy cause or people more deserving than someone like him who had killed his own mother.

His mother literally sacrificed her life for him. Mrs. O'Carroll's pregnancy was high-risk from the start, but she'd desperately wanted to have a child. She had already battled an acute bout of high blood pressure, but during the pregnancy, her body came completely undone. She was placed on bed rest after the first trimester. Her physicians advised the O'Carrolls again to terminate the pregnancy because it could be fatal. Mr. O'Carroll pleaded with his wife to follow the directions of her doctor and a few neonatal specialists who were flown in from California, but he knew it would be better to be on team baby than sitting on the bench with no wife and child.

By the time Liam was surgically removed from his mother's stomach, Mrs. O'Carroll looked malnourished with a huge, swollen belly. His father had the best people on staff to deliver the baby, but his wife's wish to have a baby came with the ultimate sacrifice. Mr. O'Carroll held his wife's tiny hand as her life slowly drained from her frail body. A single tear of heaven fell from her sunken eyes as she heard her son cry for the first time. Mrs. O'Carroll's hand then went limp in her weeping husband's gentle grasp.

A highly paid personal nurse waited for the right moment to carefully take baby Liam from Mr. O'Carroll, who wept and held dearly to his wife's lifeless body. It was then that Mr. O'Carroll promised to spoil his son with the finest things money could afford him. It was his way of honoring his deceased wife. Unfortunately, Liam favored his mother's spirit, who had cherished the simplicity of love over money.

Liam and his father never quite had the relationship Liam had wanted. He had felt closer to the mother he never remembered meeting. He had Catherine, his mother's name, tattooed over his heart. Later, he had added a baby with outreached hands extending to the sky.

His brand-new rented silver Toyota Tundra platinum series pulled up to the front of the building. A gray, unkempt, bearded man in tattered, worn clothing climbed from out of the captain's seat. He retrieved a small grimy grocery sized plastic bag from the seat, as if he was trying to keep the soil of his clothes from getting the truck's interior dirty.

"Thank you, kind sir." Liam extended his hand towards the man of average build.

"I'm gonna call you one-of-a-kind, cause I get called many names, but sir is not one of them." The homeless man humbly bowed his head as he accepted the money in the palm of Liam's hand. "I cleaned the tires and made sure I didn't dirty your truck."

"Thanks. I'm sure all is good." Liam depressed the button to return the driver's seat back to his specific settings and then hopped in.

The appreciative man pulled opened the door for Indigo. "Ma'am, I hope you and your husband have a great day."

Indigo didn't say a word, but nodded in a gesture of thanks.

Darby had witnessed several exchanges where Liam paid homeless people, male and female, to circle busy New York City streets or valet park off the main road. He could have easily paid for parking garage fees but seemed gratified to help someone who could use a helping hand. Darby wasn't sure if he asked to see a driver's license before handing over his keys or how much he gifted them, but his motives were clear.

She was just a few feet from the truck. The scruffy man was still voicing his devotion at the thoughtful gesture. He still had the money grasped tightly in his dirty hand. It was as if he wouldn't look at it until the truck pulled off. Liam pulled the lever into drive and entered ongoing traffic. Just before the automatic door locks engaged, Darby yanked opened the rear door behind Indigo and gained access to the fully loaded truck.

"How are you doing, stranger?" Darby said with confidence.

Indigo's reflexes kicked in and she turned to greet the intruder with ill intentions, but Liam's response assured her that they weren't in any imminent danger.

"Darby, how the hell are you?" Liam didn't seem surprised at her unexpected arrival. "It's been a long time."

"Yeah, too long." Darby never answered how she was doing. Instead, she directed her attention to Indigo. "Hi, I know the Irish meathead driving, but I don't know you."

Indigo didn't speak, but raised her fist in the air. Darby shrugged to Liam as if to say, "What's up with her?"

Keeping an eye on the slow-moving traffic and the women in his truck, Liam said, "Darby, this is Indigo. Indigo, this is Darby. The woman who I told you Noah was lost without." He paused briefly before speaking again. "Darby, Indigo doesn't talk."

In an apologetic tone, Darby said, "Oh, I didn't know." She then leaned forward in her seat and yelled, "HI, MY NAME IS DARBY. IT'S GOOD TO MEET YOU!"

"No. No. Please don't do that." Liam tried to stop Darby before she pissed off Indigo. "I said she doesn't talk. I didn't say she couldn't hear."

By then, Indigo was rocking in her seat, trying to keep her composure. She knew they were still in New York because they needed to know what happened to Noah, the man Liam called a brother. Strangely, she was committed to whatever Liam needed her to do.

Darby didn't allow her embarrassment to thwart her mission; small talk was done. "I know who killed Noah."

Two sets of ears twitched like satellites receiving information, but there was complete silence in the truck. The two occupants waited to hear more from Darby.

"The people who did it are still breathing." She got choked up but managed to continue on. "And shouldn't be."

Liam pounded his fist into his other hand and stretched his neck from side to side before speaking. "Take us to them. Now!"

Darby was taken back a bit by his response. It wasn't just that he was ready to seek revenge, but how willing Indigo seemed as well. The woman she knew very little about was ready to fight for Noah; a man she didn't know. Darby didn't allow her bewilderment to show as she spoke matter-of-factly.

"Not now. I have a meeting I must attend, but I'll be in touch."

"Take my number," Liam offered.

"Have it already. Just make sure you pick up when I call," Darby said.

"Resourceful, like when we were kids." Liam grinned.

"I guess some things don't change." Darby allowed a quick smirk to come through. "My SUV is back by the restaurant. Wait, the chip? Noah's was in his hand. And yours?"

Indigo was completely in the dark. She wondered what chip Darby was referring to and if Liam had any clue. She didn't have to wait long to know.

"Behind my left ear," Liam stated. "The promise Noah and I made to our fathers." He shook his head in disgust. "They didn't need to put a stupid implant in us. Noah was my brother without it. I'm going to punish those who killed him."

Darby was satisfied with the meeting. She sat back in her seat and contemplated some more about the speechless woman. "What's her deal? She has no skin in this fight. Even if she's in love with Liam, is she willing to die for his childhood friend?" Darby chuckled to herself. "I guess. I've arrested women for doing stupider things for their boos—romantic fools."

"Tell me what happened to Noah." Liam's words shook Darby from her thoughts.

Darby had a rehearsed story she told the Bureau of how Chameleon and his goons had conspired to take out an undercover New York detective squad and how Noah was in the wrong place at the wrong time, but Liam deserved the truth. Her fabricated sequence of events of that awful night made it just a bit easier to handle Noah's murder.

"They set him up. He thought he was doing g ... oo ... d." Darby's words stopped being recognizable. She was overwhelmed by a storm of sobbing. Thoughts of what truthfully happened to the love of her life, and the secret she didn't get the chance to tell him about their beautiful daughter, exploded all at once.

Liam pulled some leftover, brownish, recycled fast-food napkins from underneath the arm console. He handed them back to Darby, refusing to look directly at her. Indigo put her fingers in her ears. She desperately tried to block out Darby's cries. When that didn't have the effect she wanted, Indigo curled into a ball. She recognized Darby's injured spirit.

The truth of what happened that night would have to be told when Darby was ready. Darby was still a mess when she finally got back to her SUV.

CHAPTER 11: SORRY

Indigo Martinez grew up with both her mother and father in the city of Los Angeles. She was one of five children. Her parents raised their four boys and little princess with love and respect. Indigo was the second youngest and, being the only girl, was the jewel of her father's eye. The family would joke that it was at birth she first had her father wrapped around her tiny finger. The two of them were inseparable. He went to dance recitals and helped her practice her cheerleading routines without giving it a second thought. Although he managed to spread his time around to each of his children, it was undeniable that Indigo was his tagalong.

Mrs. Martinez was the traditional soccer mom and the constant figure at all of her boys' practices and games. She taught second grade at the local public elementary school. Her weekends were consumed with doing lesson plans, cooking, and hollering at referees for missing penalties against her sons' teams. She had always managed to avoid being tossed from the field. Although her words were never too vulgar, it was her slim, curvy Hispanic beauty that kept her on the sidelines. Mrs. Martinez had the goods that had men adoring her, and women wishing they were her.

As the years passed, Indigo began to look more and more like her mother. By the age of ten, boys three grade levels older than her were constantly seeking her attention. Luckily, knowledge she had four brothers was widespread throughout the community, so her pursuers came at her with respect. Her brothers didn't allow any boy to get too close to their sister, which wasn't a big deal because at that time she didn't have any interest in boys.

Indigo's eldest brother, who enjoyed high school wrestling and karate, made it his mission in life to teach his baby sister how to fight. At first, she tried to avoid him, but her father suggested she learn. There was no way she would disappoint her father, so she gave it her all. It wasn't an easy task because her brother didn't pull punches. He pounded on her as if she was his equal. Her bruises went away, but her toughness and fighting skills grew in leaps and bounds.

By fifteen, she had out worked most boys on the co-ed soccer team and hung up her blue and gold pompoms for lacrosse gloves and a stick. Her coach would repeatedly remind her to grab a helmet to practice in, but secretly loved her grit. Both her high school soccer and lacrosse teams had unusually filled stands with not only athletes' parents but also spectators who came to see the hardcore bombshell known as I.M. or Instant Madness.

Indigo's brothers never displayed any jealously about the fame and notoriety their sister received in school or the community. Actually, sibling association perks came their way too—*muchas muchachas*. Life for the Martinez family was one to be treasured.

At sixteen, Indigo had been studying with Mario, the boy next door. Both families practically considered each other as blood cousins. Mario was the same age and in many of the same classes in high school. He was a smart, scrawny kid with only a handful of friends. He never minded his lack of friends and status at school because Mario had the attention of his secret crush.

Sadly for him, Indigo had him as far back in the friend zone a boy could be that it was odd he didn't suffer from nosebleeds. He also flew under the radar of her brothers. They saw him as a harmless squirt of a tutor who they weren't even sure liked girls.

Mario dreamed about Indigo and him being together for years, but never had the courage to share his intentions. He was content with spending time in her bedroom, sitting on the bed she slept in at night, and cherished whenever she touched him as she laughed at one of his unoriginal jokes that he borrowed off the Internet.

During a routine study session in Indigo's room, Mario sat at her desk. He was trying to busy himself with the Calculus problem, but that day Indigo was looking exceptionally beautiful. To his senses, her perfume was as alluring as lilac to a honeybee. She leaned down over him. Her luscious, long black hair flowed over his shoulder and parts of its ends tickled his ear and face. Mario struggled to recall a formula to solve the math problem because his focus was on his crush. Beads of sweat appeared on his forehead and his armpits heated up, triggering his forty-eight-hour deodorant to do as advertised.

"One. Two. Three." Mario mentally counted off before breaking free from his fears. He turned around and kissed the startled girl of his dreams on the lips.

Crunch!

"*Estas loco.*" Indigo reacted with a solid, well-placed punch to his left eye and cheekbone. Instinctively, she recoiled into her fighting stance with her fists readied to strike again.

"Sorry. Sorry." Mario sat down, stunned by what had just happened. His eyes were a blink away from releasing the welled-up tears.

Indigo caught her reflection in her mirror. Ashamed, she lowered her hands and relaxed her posture. She stared at Mario, trying to go back to solving the math problem. A small red lump had already formed on his cheek. His legs were shaking. Indigo could tell he wanted to take flight. She tried to say something apologetically, but he quickly gathered up his things in one swift swoop and exploded out of her room. She watched him from her window, dropping his stuff as he frantically wiped tears away.

As her front door slammed close, Indigo felt her long childhood friendship coming to a close, too. She had trouble sleeping that night. Indigo rehearsed her lines until she was overcome with exhaustion. In the morning, her plan was to meet Mario at his locker and apologize until he said everything was okay.

Two days passed before Indigo heard that Mario's parents had called him out sick without a date of return. She had attempted several texts and phone calls, but Mario didn't respond or accept any of them. At one point, she had thought about baking him his favorite double-layered chocolate fudge brownies with no nuts, but it ended up being a fleeting thought. Instead, her time was consumed with friends, sports, and a loving, bustling family.

It had been more than seven days since Indigo had seen or heard from Mario. Her conscience about making things right was now in overdrive. She spent her Saturday morning prepping the fudge brownies while fighting off her greedy brothers. Indigo packaged the brownies in a red plastic wrapper. It was midday when she went over to Mario's home. His mother greeted Indigo like she was her own daughter returning from college.

"Good. He didn't tell her what happened," Indigo thought.

"Mario! Indigo is here to see you." His mother yelled up the stairs. "He's going to be so happy you came over." A minute or two passed, but Mario still hadn't come down. "It's alright. You can go up."

"Uh. I'd like to surprise him. Do you mind getting him?" Indigo wanted to make amends for her huge mistake, but was afraid to face Mario alone.

"Of course. I can't wait to see his face when he sees you." Mario's mother grabbed a small laundry basket before going to corral her son.

Indigo was anxious. Her nerves had her fingers twitching. She checked her phone and noticed an email from Mario that had come in about thirty minutes earlier. It was titled *SORRY*. She took in a deep breath, but didn't get a chance to read that email.

"No! *Mi hijo!*" His mother cried out for her son.

The screams that came from Mario's room told her something was horrifically wrong. Mario's father bolted from the family room to go check on his hysterical wife. Once he made it to the room, cries from him could be heard, but Mario's mother's ear-piercing shrieks were as if someone was ripping her apart.

Indigo's parents had to come and physically carry her away, kicking and screaming from Mario's home. His parents prevented her from going to Mario's room and wanted her out of their house before the coroners took their son's lifeless body to the mortuary. Later, Indigo was told Mario suffered from situational depression and had stopped taking his prescribed medication. When she researched it further, she learned how Mario suffered from an adjustment disorder. Basically, he couldn't handle traumatic events like the one he'd had with her.

Indigo, the teenager who had it all, was never the same after losing her friend, especially feeling responsible for Mario taking his own life. That was the last time she had spoken to anyone.

CHAPTER 12: THERAPY

Darby was a few minutes late to her two o'clock session with the Bureau's shrink. She didn't mind her two required meetings per week. It was her free ticket away from work, so she could find those responsible for Noah's murder. Psychologist Michael Smarra, who wanted to be called Mike, was in his late twenties. He was tall and lanky. The only muscle he exercised was his brain. Behind the baby face, Cali-surfer tan, and excellent conversationalist abilities, Mike was one of the best in his field. If you asked him or just gave it time, he'd tell you he was the best the FBI had to offer.

When Mike wasn't busy proving if someone was sane or too insane to continue to work for the Bureau, he did night work as a criminal profiler. He found in pleasure developing psychological profiles, analyzing mounds of evidence, and studying human behaviors and characteristics.

"Special Agent Rice, I didn't think you were coming."

Darby knew Mike was waiting for a reaction, so she calmly blamed her unprecedented tardiness on New York traffic. She was always on guard the minute she was ever in his company. Darby didn't want to appear fixed after taking a shotgun blast to the chest, but also didn't want to appear so broken she would be forced out of the FBI. She needed more time to execute her plan to take down Tyrus, Big 60, and the strange one.

"Please, this is our fourth session now, and I insist you call me Darby. Besides, isn't it your job to make me feel comfortable so I can share my deepest, darkest thoughts?"

Mike's head tilted slightly to the left as if he was calculating the risk factor of calling a client by first name only. "Do you think it's your darkest secrets I'm after?" He sidestepped her request with his usual way of answering a question by asking a question.

"No, I didn't say anything about secrets. You did." Darby was on her game.

Mike took a sip of water from a glass with the image of baby Yoda on it before peppering Darby with three decisive questions. "Are you back with your family? Have you let the water flow freely?" Mike set a tissue contained in a miniature Millennium Falcon spacecraft on the table closer to Darby. Then he asked his third question. "Are you ready to return to duty?" He relaxed his posture, crossed his legs at the ankles, and waited to record Darby's verbal and nonverbal responses.

"No, I haven't been home. But I FaceTime them regularly," Darby lied without allowing any of her body twitches to say otherwise.

"Do you think you're still in danger? Should the Bureau know of others?" Mike said it like he cared one way or the other about the answers to his recent inquiries.

"No, again. I'm either not sleeping or having nightmares." That was the truth. "I don't want my family to know that I'm still having trouble coping with what happened."

"Can you tell me what happened?" Mike had asked this question over twenty times.

"Of course I can. Google it. The Brooklyn Blitz was major headlines." Darby's voice cracked. "News of what happened is for all to read."

Mike saw an opening and took it. "Downpours can be very therapeutic." With his eyes, he pointed towards the Millennium Falcon.

"I've had my moments, but not what you described would happen." She told another lie. Although Darby felt better than she had in weeks, the uncontrollable downpour of emotions and tears that happened in Liam's truck wasn't anything she was ready to share with her shrink. "Trust me. I'll tell you if it does."

"May the force be with you," the alarm clock sounded.

"Special Agent Rice, indulge me. Are you ready to go back to duty?"

"Mike, I'm ready when you say I'm ready." Darby appealed to his larger-than-life ego of being the best.

"Thank you for having confidence in me." He grinned. "Rightly so, but ultimately it will be you who will let me know when you're ready to return. Until then, your homework assignment will be to go see your family. You can't do this alone. Besides, when you do return, expect your new assignment to be as far away from New York as you can imagine."

"I'm not alone. I have you. Right?" Darby said in a flirtatious manner.

"See you next week, Special Agent Rice."

LaWayne Williams

That night Darby spent hours Face Timing her parents and daughter. Afterwards, she slept well for the first time in about a month.

CHAPTER 13: FRIENDS

Location: New York two-bedroom hotel suite

"What happened back there?" Liam wanted answers that he'd tried to get in the past, but this time it could mean life or death.

Indigo pulled a pocket-sized notepad from her rear pocket. She used golf like pencils with AB grade lead for darker bold strokes as her writing tools. She found it easier to communicate with others this way. The only issue was the smudges it left on her hands.

She wrote, *"Nothing."*

"What do you mean nothing? I saw you. There is something wrong, and it's time you fess up." Liam tried to remain calm, but his Irish temper was who he was—passionate.

Indigo attempted to walk away, but Liam grabbed her by the arm. Her heavily worn, faded blue baseball cap with the letters AF embroidered in the center shook loose from her head. Liam managed to catch it before it fell to the floor.

"Sorry, I know how much the hat means to you," Liam said sympathetically.

The hat was Mario's. He'd wanted to be an Air Force pilot. During one of their studying nights, he had left it in Indigo's bedroom. Mario planned to get it back, but after seeing Indigo wearing it, he secretly conjured up in his head that her having the hat meant they were a couple.

"Wow! I've never seen your hair this long before." Liam stared admiringly at Indigo.

Usually, she kept her hair cut in a close tomboyish style, but she didn't know they'd be in New York for so long, so her luscious black hair grew freely. Indigo snatched the hat from Liam's grasp and crushed it back onto her head. Feeling a bit uncomfortable at the way Liam was looking at her, she forgot to pull her hair back into a ponytail. Her hair sprouted down from under her hat, covering parts of her face too.

Still gazing at Indigo, as if seeing her beauty for the first time, Liam gently moved hair away from her eyes. "You should keep your hair long."

Indigo had been told she was a ten since she knew what it meant, so Liam's reaction was classic. She had tried to tone down her sex appeal to others by masking it with less than flattering boyish clothes, no makeup, and close-cut hair. Frankly, Indigo could model a beekeeper's suit with helmet and slick rubber gloves and still be the queen of the hive.

"Do you know I care about you?" Liam spoke from his heart.

Indigo was used to watching Liam pick up fast women at bars or groupies willing to do anything, but now his eyes were dancing with hers as his mouth spoke smooth words.

"And I you." She had her fair share of relationships with men, but her friendship with Liam was similar to the one she had with Mario.

"Bad things are about to happen." Liam paused but didn't take his eyes off her. "Things you won't be able to undo. I should've said no to you coming with me."

"You did! But I ignored you." She ripped the page from the notepad and let it fall to the floor. On the next empty sheet she wrote, *"Friends!"*

Indigo knew all too well how men despised being placed in the friend zone, but she felt that was less creepy than writing family. She wasn't naïve to the on and off attraction they'd had. Yet neither one acted on any of the pleasurable impulses.

Like kryptonite to the fictional hero Superman, reading what Indigo wrote freed him from the hypnotic stare down. "Yes, we're friends, but you don't owe me nothing. Tomorrow you go back to Cali," Liam demanded.

"Hell no!" she wrote with broad strokes.

Liam punched a sizable hole in the hotel wall. "You're acting like a tool! You go back tomorrow. That's final!"

"You can't boss me around." Indigo tore off another sheet of paper and gave Liam a solid, two-handed shove to his massive chest.

Her action was unexpected, but he managed to quickly regain his balance without falling.

"Technically, I am your boss. And friend too. So, as your friend and best boss, I'm demanding that you leave in the morning. You don't owe me nothing."

She repeatedly wrote, *"Friends! Friends! Friends!"* The more she wrote it, the more she envisioned Mario. The guilt of him taking his own life resurfaced and began to put a stranglehold on her emotions.

"Listen! You don't owe me anything," Liam shouted.

"I'm sorry. I'm so sorry."

A bewildered Liam said, "Sorry for what?"

Indigo wasn't herself as her thoughts and emotions collided violently with one another. "I won't leave you alone again."

She dropped her notepad to the floor. Then she busied her hands by beating on Liam's chest. Eventually, he was able to restrain her by her wrists. The two of them locked eyes before sharing the long-awaited teenage Mario and Indigo kiss. Only seconds in, the kiss brought Indigo back to her senses. She broke free from Liam's grasp and stormed into the bathroom.

"Please come out?" Liam pleaded. "Let's talk about what just happened."

Indigo grabbed Liam's razor from the sink. She stared hard at her reflection in the oval-shaped mirror. Liam's disturbing cries for her to open the door bounced from wall to wall. Indigo tried to drown out what he was saying by turning on the bathroom exhaust fan. But the upscale bathroom fan gently whispered as it spun.

In the morning, Liam grabbed a protein drink from the mini-fridge. He downed it in one deep gulp. He tossed the empty carton into a small trashcan that he suddenly noticed was filled with luscious black hair.

"Hair or no hair, you're still a stunner!" Liam yelled in the direction of Indigo's room. "You'll just have to live with that!"

Indigo smiled as she continued to do her morning routine of leg raised push-ups from her elevated hotel bed.

CHAPTER 14: GATECRASHER

Whisper returned to his surveillance duties at his ex-wife's home. The familiar voices coming from the home comforted his spirit. The assassination of the dirty cop didn't bother him, but living as a loner to protect those he loved was getting old. He closed his eyes to enhance his sense of hearing. His daughter's laughter almost covered up the sound of the footsteps of five heavily armed intruders.

Intruder One appeared to be giving the orders. He singled with his hands for the other four to take their positions. Two casually walked to the rear of the home. The last two nonchalantly went to either side of the home. With the gun at the ready, Intruder One rang the doorbell and waited to kill the first person to open the door.

"Amateurs," Whisper thought. "The leader will be last."

Typically, one hired gunman would strike fear in most men's hearts and five would send them into cardiac arrest. However, Whisper saw it as live target practice.

"I determine who lives or dies. Today you're bait." Whisper took aim at the heavy one, who was standing guard on the side of the house. He put a bullet in his leg.

"Uh! Help meeeeee!" The heavy gunman didn't disappoint as he cried out to the others. "I'm hit!"

"Pathetic." Whisper didn't have to wait long before dropping another gunman who ran from the other side of the house to help his chunky friend. The helper wasn't so fortunate, as his life was quickly taken.

Whisper watched as Intruder One forced his way through the front door while the two at the rear of the home took cover and returned fire. They shot in many directions except the one where Whisper hid.

"Tisk. Tisk. You've been naughty," a voice came from behind Whisper who was still lying in a prone position.

"I guess they call you the Gatecrasher." Whisper surmised the sixth intruder was to crash the party after shots were fired.

"Ha. Ha. Name calling with a 9mm pointed at the back of your head. Ballsy." Gatecrasher was intoxicated with power and drunk with words. "I don't see nothing dangerous about you. Actually, the only thing I see is a dead man." Gatecrasher kicked dirt onto the back of Whisper's camouflage pants. "I know people in our business have a code. So I'll give you a chance to go out with some dignity. Try your luck. Go for the gun in your waistband or wait until my boss drags your daughter out by her hair, begging for her life."

Whisper had heard what he needed. Gatecrasher was just a pawn. His first instinct was correct. Intruder One held the information he needed. He slowly took his hands away from the rifle. With outstretched palms, he extended his arms away from his body.

"Come on, man. Really?" Gatecrasher was disappointed by Whisper's choice. "Cowardly move."

Click.

That was the last sound Gatecrasher heard. The rigged gadget Whisper called *Got My Six*, two remote triggered automatic assault rifles, had Gatecrasher's body doing the dance of death. Whisper leaped to his feet, grabbed Gatecrasher's 9mm, and headed towards the back of the house.

The two men left to put up a fight were no match for an experienced gunman who was determined to intercept Intruder One. Whisper wounded both hired killers before walking up at point blank range to finish the job. One man received a round to the back of the head as he tried to crawl away.

Meanwhile, Intruder One had finally gained access to the main bedroom. He fired two shots into the mass that was covered up by the teal bed comforter. He was given specific instructions to confirm all kills. He yanked the comforter off the bed and was surprised to see a dummy wrapped up in the sheets. As soon as he realized it was a trap, he had a 9mm muzzle against his head.

"Drop it and you might have a chance to live." Whisper hoped he'd get a chance to get information from Intruder One, but was more than willing to put a bullet in his head.

Intruder One let his gun slip free from his hands. "I see you've been expecting us."

Whisper had actually expected professionals not college kids for hire. It was like whomever set up the hit had solicited a diversified frat house. Intruder One was in his early twenties, Hispanic, and had a thin, boyish face and a slight accent.

With his chest puffed out, Intruder One said, "I'm not afraid to die."

Whisper knew he was bluffing, because if he really wasn't scared, he would not had dropped the gun. "Tell me what I need and I promise I'll make it quick."

"You're a dead man talking." Intruder One had fire in his eyes.

Whisper glanced over his shoulder and returned his attention with malice in his voice. "You sound almost as confident as the last guy who tried to sneak up on me. If you're waiting for him, he's not coming."

Intruder One seemed to lose his rugged edge, but then quickly appeared to have made the decision to die with honor.

An hour later

Intruder One, whose name was Steven, resisted thirty minutes longer than what Whisper had anticipated. His lifeless body showed the evidence of torture. He finally broke and told Whisper everything he needed. The conductor paid by the late Chameleon to organize the hit on Whisper's family was Steven's cousin, Pedro. He gave up his home address and places Pedro frequently visited.

Whisper knew he only had about twelve to fifteen hours before Pedro realized something had gone wrong. He spent two hours disposing of the bodies in a large pre-dug hole. Whisper removed all of their identifications for insurance purposes. If he didn't get to Pedro in time, the casualty count would set records. Whisper was willing to do anything to keep his loved ones safe. The last thing he did before setting the house ablaze was carefully removing the flash drive that contained the recording of his ex-wife and daughter's voices. He had convinced them to relocate about a month ago.

CHAPTER 15: PERMISSION

Kate sat in bed with her legs crossed at the ankles and her back against the metal headboard. Concealed files of the Brooklyn Blitz occupied the space around her. She was intent on finding something, but she had no clue what it was.

Tia had pulled some strings and collected a few favors just to get twenty-four hours to review four large office boxes of evidence collected from that horrific day. She had no interest in reliving the case, but would do anything for the woman she loved.

"Why don't you give it a break for now?" Tia pleaded with Kate.

"Not yet. Besides, we have to give it back soon and I still haven't found what I needed," Kate said, without taking her eyes off the paper she was reading.

Tia didn't want Detective Lawson. She wanted Kate, her lover.

Frustrated at not finding any leads, especially one that would name her shooter, Kate threw papers to the floor. "Damn. I'm just not good enough."

Tia ran her fingers through her lover's short hair. "You got this. You're one of the sharpest detectives I've seen."

Kate tried to battle against relentless flashbacks of her cowering behind a dumpster while Detective Nine, her mentor, fought alone to save her life. "You don't know what I know. I'm ashamed to be here."

"Don't talk like that. You're just struggling with survivor's remorse," Tia tried to console her. "It will do you some good to walk away from it for a while. Come here. I'll make you forget those silly papers."

"Silly? Really? People were murdered!" At close range, Kate aimed her frustrations intentionally towards Tia. "Your cousin was killed. Was she silly, too?"

"Nope! Not this time. My tip toeing days around your erratic feelings are done." Tia took a step back from the bed and threw her hands up in the air.

"Maybe you're right. We should press pause on our—"

"Stop with your White girl way of breaking up." Tia was completely fed up.

"Oh, we're bringing race into this." Kate rose from the bed.

"Not race, just your constant attempt to throw our love away. Show me you have a backbone and tell me why you want to be done with me. Cause I'm done ice-skating around your frozen feelings for me." Tia had said her piece and waited for Kate to respond. She tried to prepare her heart for the worst.

"So, you want me to go *sister* on you?" Kate did air quotes with her fingers. She rolled her eyes and head as she spoke. "Well, I can't stand the way you touch me. It's like having a senile uncle asking you for a hug and he feels you up at the end. And kissing you makes my skin crawl and I have to keep from throwing up. And your smell …" Kate was starting to lose control of her emotions. Tears ran down her face. "You smell like her. You changed your perfume to hers. What's up with that? I have to not only look at a face that resembles hers but have to smell her damn perfume too! By the way, I've only kept you around to stay close to the Brooklyn Blitz case. Now, is that *sister* enough for you?"

Tia felt like she had just been punched in the throat. Her heart sank hard in her chest. Feeling a dizzy spell coming on, she took a seat on the chair next to the bed. Tia put her head in her lap and hands over her head. What happened next was like someone had given her two EpiPen injections.

"Kate, I know I should be sympathetic to you and probably say something endearing to comfort your fragile spirit, but I just need you to know, YOU … GOT … THE … WRONG … ONE … TODAY." Tia rose to her feet with fight in her eyes. "Don't let my job and pant suits fool you. You about to get a Jersey City beat down—Greenville all day!"

"What does where you live have to—"

Tia's sudden body jerk towards her interrupted Kate. The aggressive move startled her. Until that day, the two of them had only had a handful of verbal spats, but Kate knew Tia was struggling not to lose control. She smartly decided to listen and only speak when asked or told to.

46

An angry, frustrated Tia exploded with her own truthful words. "I thought I did something to you! You know, like I said something that hurt your feelings, flirted with someone at work, or didn't give you enough attention." Tia pounded one fist into the palm of her other hand. "No! My cousin sacrificed her life to save yours. And the thanks for that is you want to kill our relationship. I thought I had done something wrong. You made me feel like I somehow wronged you. But no! You are fighting demons in your head instead of fighting for us. Damn, you!"

Tia closed the distance between the two of them and Kate tensed up with nervous anticipation.

"I don't give you permission to end our relationship. And I'm done tiptoeing around your feelings. This *sister* never took ballerina lessons and I don't plan on starting." Tia held out her hand. "I'm done waiting for you to let me in, too. I'm no stranger. Give me back the damn house key!"

Kate scrambled across her bed and reached into the small lamp drawer. She kept her eyes on Tia as she shifted clumsily through her underwear until she found the single brass key. It was attached to a tiny beach sandal with the word Bahamas stitched down the center. Kate reached her hand out for Tia to retrieve the key. Tia grabbed Kate's hand and pulled the two of them so close that their noses were practically touching.

"I'll go back to my original perfume, but my face is what I was born with and it's damn fine, if you ask me." Tia took the key from Kate's hand but didn't step back. Instead she gave Kate a firm slap on her butt. "And the next time I pat you on your ass at work, you better say, 'Lieutenant, may I have another?'"

Kate had a strong urge to laugh, but under the circumstances she wisely resisted. She didn't know if Tia had regained full control of her emotions yet. Besides, the slap she received on her ass from Tia had some bite to it. It definitely bordered on a love tap and an all-out physical assault. Kate could smell the Rivata Casa Rossa red wine on Tia's breath as she continued to speak.

"I asked myself if I was with you because you were the last person with my cousin. But I didn't have to think for long. I'm with you because my heart needs to be fed by your love. It's hungry for only you."

Tia tilted her head slightly, leaned in a little and kissed Kate on the lips. It wasn't a lingering kiss, but long enough for Kate to feel the tears flowing from Tia's swollen eyes. Her adrenaline had run its course, and now she was an emotional mess.

Tia attempted to wipe away tear with her hands before speaking again. "I need to go and you need to fight for us."

Kate closed her eyes and tensed up in anticipation for another whack on her butt, but it never came. When she opened her eyes, she saw Tia running around the room, grabbing her essential belongings until her hands couldn't hold anything else. Then she dashed out of the bedroom door.

"Argh!" Kate was exasperated with her failed attempts to spare Tia's feelings. She knew the words she said could never be taken back and at that point, she didn't care. At any cost, she would find the sniper, even if it meant endangering her own life again. She didn't want to have someone to live for and love. Kate slammed and threw things around the room until she finally screamed into a pillow, "I'll change the LOCKS!"

"I wish you would!" Tia said with hurt in her voice when she returned to the room.

Kate pulled her face away from the pillow. She tried to control her breathing, but her body was still strongly heaving in and out from the effects of her mini-tantrum.

"A friend in high places told me there's an agent who witnessed many of the murders. She's still in the city getting her head examined." Tia tossed a piece of paper on the bed with a name on it. "That's the name of her shrink."

Kate had finally gotten her big break in the case. Overwhelmed with excitement, Kate patted the bed for Tia to join her. She stared seductively at Tia and said, "Lieutenant, may I have another?"

"I'll take a rain check. You hurt me tonight."

CHAPTER 16: KEEPER

There were three people sitting in a room absent of color and things that could bring it to life. The space was built to be the family room of a modest residential home set in East Orange, New Jersey. The lack of style and decorum was actually appropriate for its purpose. The room was a holding area for short meetings, stashing products, or evading capture.

Tyrus had ordered Big 60 to secure safe houses from New York to Florida and even one in the Virgin Islands. In total, there were seven, and four were in operation. He relied on his military training to scope out and setup each place. Buildings varied from a barn off the beaten path to a bustling complex with varied shops and health care services.

A single mother of two small children occupied the East Orange 1,500 square foot home. Big 60 found the woman at a shelter for battered women. He promised her free rent and protection from her kids' insanely abusive father. In return, she couldn't ask any questions and stayed out of the holding area room. Her reason to run four states away from her tormentor was to keep her kids safe, so she jumped at his offer. It had been almost been a year since she had a close encounter with the monster that routinely visited her in nightmarish dreams. Big 60 never told her he had already snapped the neck of an angry man waiting in a beat-up car outside the shelter where he found her. Big 60 banked on her fear and desperation for security for her absolute loyalty.

Although the safe house was hardly visited by anyone from Tyrus's crew, she wisely kept out of sight whenever someone did show up. Her two- and three-year-old girls were always in the mood for a spontaneous game of hide and seek in their mother's bedroom or a sleepover at a trusted friend's house.

As a redhead with fair skin and a natural athletic physique, beauty dangled at the ends of each of the curls on her head. Her battered self-esteem couldn't dim her brilliant smile nor stop men from showing interest. She avoided potential suitors but found Big 60's dominant presence not only safe but also appealing. She was too shy to reveal her attraction to him. As the keeper of the safe house, she could only wish that one day he would truly see her for the first time.

Big 60 had a mutual fondness for her too, but had only sworn to protect her. So he kept his feelings for her hidden. He knew loving anyone would ultimately bring chaos, strife, or worse—death. He had nurtured his male desires with women of the night and those who bar hopped for just a good time, but he knew she was neither. She was someone to marry, raise a family, and grow old with. Big 60 made it his mission to keep her safe and secure. He paid off the East Orange home and rarely used it as a meeting place. Big 60 told her about the shallow wall in one of the kid's rooms. He told her to only look behind it if she hadn't heard from him for 90 consecutive days.

He wanted to save her the pain of thinking something bad had happened to him by telling her when that day came, it meant the safe house was compromised and it couldn't be used again. Big 60 knew she could be trusted because, through no fault of hers, her brutal life experiences had produced an obedient spirit. Her brokenness of self-worth and desire to fight for her kids was polarizing to him. He wished he had the time to help her heal, but knew he wasn't a head shrink. Instead, Big 60 did what he thought was best for her and the kids. Hidden behind the wall were the paid deeds to the home, lucrative ventures throughout the city and others, startup money, and a note that would set her free of fear from her kids' father.

Big 60 had already alerted her of the meeting and insisted she find a place to go for the night. He went as far as to tell her to not return until he sent her the cryptic all-clear signal. She didn't ask any questions because she trusted him with her life and, more importantly, she knew Big 60 would keep her kids safe.

CHAPTER 17: CORD

Tyrus was to lead the evening's meeting. It was the first one where he would bark orders at Big 60 in the presence of others. Big 60 didn't want to chance what Tyrus would want to do to the keeper and her kids, or what he would have to do to his childhood friend.

Big 60 sat patiently on a black leather chair, watching his two protégés. He was so proud of how far they'd come up in the organization. Just like the keeper, he had given nicknames to the two other physical bodies in the room. Big 60 christened Chesa - Rip and Jason - Cord. Together, they were like the cord that was pulled to release a parachute—they protected one another.

Rip and Cord embraced their names like they'd had them since birth. Each had their name tattooed on their trigger finger. At first, Big 60 was furious they'd do something so blatantly stupid by self-identifying themselves to the police, but remembered he didn't recruit them because they were completely rational.

Cord was the first to be welcomed to the crew. It was by happenstance the two met. Cord, a gangly twenty-three-year-old street corner beggar, caught Big 60's attention by doing the one thing that made him an odd duck. He was having a full-blown conversation with someone only he could see and hear. Cord was possibly an undiagnosed sufferer from schizotypal personality disorder.

His mother was committed to a mental hospital when he was five years old. With no father listed on his birth certificate, and no close relative willing to take in a kid with paranoid ideas and a nonexistent personality, Cord became a ward of the state. He bounced from one foster parent to the next until aging out of the system at eighteen. His unstable upbringing and innate lack of personal skills intensified his desire to have someone safe to talk to—himself. The image that Cord saw was of himself and the voice inflection and tone was the same, but that was it. The friend he unconsciously conjured up in his mind liked to be called Mel and was a complete daredevil who lived mostly on the edge of life. Mel never disagreed with Cord, nor tried to reason through risky decisions. On the contrary, he was Cord's official hype man who suffered from acute ADHD.

Honk! Honk!

While the two of them were having their typical causal conversation between friends, Big 60 was heavy-handed on his car horn. If it hadn't been for the sharp sun glare that flashed in Cord's eyes, he would have still been oblivious to the real world. Cord gave the universal hand gesture that he didn't want to be bothered.

"Come with me if you want your life to change," barked Big 60.

Cord was set to walk off as quickly as he could, but Mel held his hand out to stop him from moving.

"Do you trust me?" Mel paced with excitement as he thought of what to say next.

"You know I do." Cord swiped his hands down his unshaved face. "You're my best friend."

Mel chirped like a parrot on caffeine, "Friends to the end. Friends to the end." Then he pointed to the stranger. "Another friend. Another friend."

Cord sauntered slowly over to the stranger's vehicle. He stopped awkwardly at the driver's side. He thought about retreating, but felt Mel's hand on his back nudging him forward. The next thing he knew, he was sitting comfortably on the plush leather seat.

As a gesture of good faith, Big 60 bounded from his car with chauffer-like hustle. He opened the rear door behind his seat. He held it opened long enough for Mel to take his seat and strap on his seatbelt. The gesture settled Cord's nerves and lit a fire under Mel's seat. He was like a puppy riding in a car for the first time.

Once back in the vehicle, Big 60 turned his attention to the nervous young man. "So, what's your name?"

"I'm Mel and that's Jason," Mel said as he freed himself from the seatbelt. He slid back and forth across the backseat.

Cord squirmed in his seat but didn't utter a word.

"If I'm not overstepping or anything, who's sitting in the back seat?" Big 60 asked.

"I'm Mel. I'm Mel!" He kicked the back of Jason's seat. "Don't just sit there. Tell him my name."

A bit agitated, Jason said, "I will, but first stop kicking my seat!" He waited a moment to be sure Mel did what he requested. Then, without making eye contact, he said, "That's Mel. He's happy to meet you."

As if he could see Mel sitting in the backseat, Big 60 looked in the rearview window and replied, "Mel, it's a pleasure to meet you."

Mel sat back and relished the fact someone other than Jason had acknowledged his existence. "Jason, I like him."

CHAPTER 18: RIP

Big 60 took pleasure in having a younger protégé. For several weeks, he kept Jason and Mel a secret from Tyrus. At first, he thought he was ready to put his manipulation skills to practice, but Jason greedily feasted on Big 60's gritty lifestyle. Whenever Big 60 suggested or commanded him to do something, Jason would either rush to do it or be nudged in the back by Mel to follow through with the request.

Although Big 60 enjoyed having a shadow half his size in bulk that stood a full three inches taller, following him around everywhere, he needed Jason to function on his own or at least find him someone other than Mel to keep him from losing his shit from time to time. The street meds he had got for Jason helped with his bouts of anxiety and depression, but he still frequently visited la-la land.

Jason was a misfit like Big 60 saw himself. It bonded them together almost more than his servitude to Tyrus. He painstakingly found the appropriate apartment complex in Jersey City, New Jersey, where questions weren't asked; Mel could exist without anyone taking advantage of Jason; and public transportation was readily available. Big 60 didn't scare easily, but it only took one trial to realize Jason behind the wheel of a car was frightening beyond measure.

Jason had what it took to be a good soldier. He was obedient, had no family, was loyal, fearless, and didn't require much to be satisfied with his cut from the street business. He had proven himself by going on some trips to crack some heads, move guns, and transport money.

"But could he take a life?" Big 60 consistently wondered.

Big 60 found humor in gang movies and television shows in which murder was the preferred appetite of the leading gangster. It served a purpose, but actually the fear of dying was what sustained criminal organizations. He had to prepare Jason for the ultimate duty as a soldier without the cliché of actually doing it without a cause. Big 60 wasn't a saint, only taking a life when it was called for, but unknowingly helping Tyrus kill his brother Noah had gone against his codes of honor.

He arranged for Jason to spend four twelve-hour days at a local butcher distributer. Big 60 paid off the owner and gave specific instructions to have Jason wielding the knives, cleavers, and saws to cut up the animal parts. Jason and Mel took to the task like lion cubs to their first meat offering.

Big 60 reviewed the security cameras that spied on the back of the butcher shop. Initially, he wanted to see how Jason handled being covered in blood and around the constant stench of raw meat, but quickly paid special attention to the last four hours of Jason's shifts.

A dark-haired Filipino woman with an average build and height became his focal point. Actually, it was how she immediately interacted with Jason and acknowledged Mel. On the first night the relationship between the two was popcorn worthy. For the first eight hours he seemed to be trying to fit in with those around him, but once the mysterious woman arrived he and Mel were free to be their true selves—uniquely strange.

Video captured her talking to Mel while she was instructing Jason on the proper way to handle a butcher's cleaver. Although they appeared to be around the same age, she seemed to have a mature grace about her.

After peppering the owner with questions, Big 60 found out her name was Chesa Flores. She was a loner, had no kids, lived about a block from Jason's apartment complex, and had a wrinkle of a scar down her right cheek. He left with a copy of the recordings before erasing the hard drive of Jason's visit. The owner's conscience seemed to realize something wasn't right, but he knew Big 60 was a dangerous man. So he graciously accepted the rest of his payment without suspicion and purged his memory of their encounter.

Big 60 moved quickly to learn more about Chesa. He watched her for several days traveling through the city in her small beat-up car and on foot. She never seemed to take the same consecutive route to her day job of servicing customers at the local coffee shop. He spent hours watching her interact with others. She appeared to force welcoming nods and smiles, but nothing was exaggerated. Her mannerisms were direct and careful. She gently dismissed advances from potential male and female suitors.

Once he had enough recon done on Chesa, he prepared to approach her. Big 60 knew he had to tread lightly without seeming demanding or intimidating. One late afternoon he followed her on foot from her day job. He was familiar with her varying patterns with her walk home so managed to follow from a distance. He cut across streets to intersect her at a less populated corner, but still have enough light to not pose a threat.

He waited for her, but strangely she never showed. Big 60 wondered if she had stopped for a last-minute item from the twenty-four-hour convenience store or she had noticed him following her and got spooked. He trekked back to his car parked blocks away in the opposite direction. To his amazement Chesa was waiting at his car.

"Do you like what you see?" Chesa said, looking directly at him.

Her choice of words, scar on her face, isolated and guarded nature had Big 60 thinking Chesa was probably a former victim of human trafficking.

He thought, "Don't mess this up." Then he responded, "It appears you know who I am."

"I do," she said matter-of-factly. She leaned comfortably against the driver's side door. "If I didn't, following me is dangerous."

Big 60 concealed his complete pleasure with what she said. "Strong words to live by."

"So, are you going to answer my question?" Chesa stood erect as if she was giving him a better look at her stature. "Do you like what you see?"

"You have potential." He knew she'd be a perfect teammate for Jason.

"Potential, huh? I'll accept that for now." Chesa walked to the other side of his car. She opened the passenger door and said, "Let's go. I'm ready for my life to change too."

CHAPTER 19: NO

Tyrus slowly opened the door to the room that was occupied by Big 60, Rip, and Cord. As if Tyrus was some kind of five-star general, Big 60 stood to show his respect. Rip and Cord sat without giving any thought to the man who had just walked into the room wearing a hockey mask.

Tyrus was pissed at their insubordination, but resisted the urge to give the order to have Big 60 exterminate them. He knew it was his idea for Big 60 to appear to be the leader of the organization while he was truly the puppet master pulling all the strings.

"Ahem," Big 60 pretended to clear his throat.

Rip stood up on cue. She pulled Cord up by tugging on a small piece of the neckline of his T-shirt.

Mel remained seated. He wasn't impressed with a grown man who walked around wearing a mask. "It's not even Halloween," Mel grumbled.

Tyrus intentionally gave his back to Rip and Cord. He wanted them to know their existence was irrelevant to him. He only spoke to Big 60.

"So, these are the newbies you were so excited about?" Tyrus's sarcasm filled the room, but fell flat on the ears of those it was directed towards.

"Yep, I'd bet my life on their loyalty," Big 60 said with complete confidence.

"I'll keep that in mind whenever they make a mistake." Tyrus wanted to assert that everyone was accountable to him. "I need you to do some weeding."

"Of course, we'll get right on it." Big 60 knew Tyrus wanted someone killed the second he walked into the room with the hockey mask. It was his signature way to express what he felt without speaking.

"No pesticides. I want you to cut straight to the roots." Tyrus wanted the hit to be messy. He handed Big 60 a wallet-sized photo.

"Aunty Cynthia?" Big 60 was shocked. "She's family. Better yet, the only one of your family left."

"She's been a mess ever since the loss of her precious Noah. Pathetic. Think of it as taking away her pain." Tyrus pretended to be sympathetic.

"No!" Big 60 sharply responded.

"I get it." Tyrus put his hand on Big 60's shoulder. "She treated you like family, but me not so much. Anyhow, I'll save you some sleepless nights and have Whisper pay her a visit."

"I said, NO!" Big 60 yelled.

Smack!

The steroids Tyrus was injecting into his thighs and buttocks had him raging madly within. His impulsive reaction to hit Big 60 across the face was only a small episode.

"Are you the Lawn Doctor now giving the orders to pulling weeds?" Tyrus said with bite.

Although Tyrus had managed to triple his size in mass and muscle, he still hadn't mastered how to apply his true force. Big 60 was more annoyed by the smack than the pain. He took his thumb and dabbed at the blood that formed at the corner of his mouth.

"Nah. I'm content with the role that I have," Big 60 said.

"Oh, hell no!" The unexpected smack sent Mel into an absolute frenzy. He paced back and forth mumbling, "Protect our friend."

Cord seemed to be holding his own. It had appeared the drugs he was taking had a strangle hold on his irrational emotions.

Tyrus threw his mask to the floor. The custom-made porcelain mask cracked down the center of the faceplate. "Do you know who you're talking to?"

"That's not good," Big 60 said under his breath.

Tyrus hardly revealed his face to anyone. Big 60 knew he had to act quickly before Tyrus did something horrible to Rip and Cord or worse—order him to do the weeding with his own gun.

"I meant no disrespect." Big 60 kneeled slowly down on one knee. He made sure Tyrus stayed focused on him. "Please find it in your heart to spare Aunty Cynthia."

"And if I don't!" Tyrus retorted.

"Then I failed you," Big 60 said in a low but purposeful whisper.

Tyrus felt threatened. His body reacted in a flight or fight response. The hairs on his arms stood up and worse, he slightly wet his pants. Embarrassed to feel fear again, he momentarily lost his mind. Tyrus went on a five-minute no breath break rant. Big 60 was careful to ignore the spit spatter that showered down on his exposed head. Each explicative was followed by saliva from his pursed lips.

"Let her memories haunt her for years to come," Big 60 interrupted.

Bonk! Bonk! Bonk!

Being interrupted was Tyrus's breaking point. He pounded his fists on Big 60's head. Big 60 refused to put up a defense. The blows rained down rapid and hard.

"What are you doing? Help our friend!" Mel pleaded with Cord. "Shoot him!"

Rip and Cord shot up from their seats. Rip was calm and focused as she looked for a signal from Big 60 to strike. Cord on the other hand, appeared moments away from doing something awful. He tried to cover his ears to drown out Mel's verbal cries to help, but Mel's words came from inside his head.

Big 60 understood the complexity of the situation. He waved off any assistance without Tyrus noticing him. Rip wasn't the issue. It was Cord who was fighting the demons within. Big 60 signaled for Rip to get control of Cord.

Tyrus was lost in utter rage to realize he was outnumbered in the room. And that the one who fed the dogs was the true master. Rip and Cord were only loyal to Big 60.

"Where is he?" Rip mouthed to Cord.

Cord, who now had one hand over one ear and the other firmly holding his gun, nodded toward the right corner of the room.

With cat like movements, Rip rushed over to that side of the room. She motioned like she had grabbed Mel, sat him down on the nearest chair, and restricted his movements by sitting on his lap.

"Umm." Mel hugged tightly to Rip. "I told you she had a thing for me." He sniffed at her hair. "She smells so gooooood."

Immediately, Cord seemed to settle down. He returned his gun to his waistband, threw his shirt over it, and took his seat again.

"She's so soft." Mel was still living out his wildest fantasies.

Tyrus's adrenaline finally slowed to a snail's crawl. He spoke with shortened breaths. "If she gets out of pocket, you mow her down. No questions asked."

Big 60 stood to his feet. His short haircut revealed signs of bruising, and his forehead was a brilliant auburn red, but still he appeared more menacing than Tyrus.

"Done." Big 60 pulled a white handkerchief from his pocket and dabbed at his busted lip again.

CHAPTER 20: DEAL

Nine hours had passed since a brutally tortured Steven was coerced into giving his last confession. Whisper was ahead of the ever-crucial ticking clock. He had kept Pedro at bay by responding with one-word texts from Steven's confiscated smartphone.

Hmm. Hmm.

Pedro's burner phone vibrated in his pocket. He quickly snatched it from his two-hundred-dollar designer jeans. He saw it was an incoming call from Steven that he listed in the phone as *ser amado,* loved one.

"*Texto? De verdad?*" Pedro spoke with a much heavier accent than Steven. "*Es mejor que tengas una buena excusa,* you better have a good excuse."

"*No hables español,* I don't speak Spanish," Whisper said bluntly.

"Who dis?" Pedro was shocked to hear someone other than his cousin's voice. "Put him on or you die."

"Sorry. Steven and his little friends are all done talking," Whisper calmly stated.

"Stefphon!" Pedro stood up from behind his oversized mahogany desk. He flipped his leather chair over. It crashed against the wall. "You dead man! Hear me? Dead!"

"Your reaction is to be expected, but I called to offer you a deal," Whisper said without emotion. "We're business men. You were just doing what you've been paid to do. Now your attempt on my family's lives and Steven's life make us even. Truce. I'm willing to move on from this."

"Funny man." Pedro cracked his neck before speaking again. "I not laughing." He swiped every family picture frame, lamp, laptop, and knickknack off his desk. Pedro went on a tirade. "You will beg me to kill you."

"*Pedro, que paso aqui?*" Pedro's wife came to investigate the noise.

Her husband was still ranting and raving too much to be understood. Pedro's wife took a single step towards her husband.

Thud!

The bullet from Whisper's rifle made quick work of Pedro's wife. She fell slowly to the floor and her body rested in place. The way her hands were under her head made it appear that she was taking a nap. Unlike the movies, there was only a small stream of blood that leaked from the hole in her forehead.

"Vera!" Pedro yelled out to his wife.

Seconds later, Junior, Pedro's teenage son, ran into his father's office. Seeing his mother laying helplessly on the floor, he rushed to her aide.

"*Mamá, levantarse!*" Junior repeatedly insisted for his mother to get up. "*Levantarse!*" He moved her hair away from her face. He went into shock on seeing her blood.

While still holding his cellphone up to one ear, Pedro used his other hand to signal for his son to stay low to the floor. Junior was in no condition to react in a normal manner. He started to get to his feet. Pedro rushed to get between his son and his office window.

"Deal! Deal!" Pedro screamed into the receiver. "You hear me? Deal!"

Whisper's second shot hit Junior in his throat. Instantly, Junior gagged on his own blood. Instinctively, he grabbed at his neck, but was about thirty-seconds from resting completely with his mother.

Pedro watched his son struggle to breathe. He felt utterly helpless. Pedro closed his eyes before grabbing from the floor a large gold-plated envelope opener. He held it like a highly skilled fighter holds a knife. He lumbered over to the large window that had two sizable holes in it, but still hadn't shattered into a million pieces.

"You want me?" Pedro yelled at the phone before violently throwing it at the overly stressed window.

Smash!

The force was too much for the window to remain intact. Large and small pieces littered inside the room and many landed outside weighing heavily on the once well-manicured bushes.

"I here!" Pedro wielded the envelope opener like a warrior against great odds.

From Whisper's vantage point, he could see a small girl who was no more than five or six caught up in her imagination as she played with stuffed animals. She was innocently unaware that she was in danger and that her family was being slaughtered. Whisper admired Pedro's courage to sacrifice his life in the hope his daughter's would be spared.

"I determine who lives or dies. Today, you die."

CHAPTER 21: THE CALL

Whisper carefully returned his rifle to the trunk of his car. Then he strolled leisurely back a block to Pedro's home. He passed a lifeless male body that was suspended between the ledge of the window and an outside bush that struggled to hold his weight. Whisper entered the house through the windowless pane. He moved with purpose to the stairs that led to the little girl's room. He removed the fitted mask that covered his face, but kept the custom-made rubber mechanic gloves on his hands.

"Hello, little one," Whisper spoke with complete kindness. "What's your name?"

"Ana," she said as she kept her attention and eyes fixed on her stuffed animals.

Up close he could see that Ana was much younger than he had first thought. He figured her young age and naïve experiences were the reasons she was receptive to a stranger that just showed up in her bedroom. His times playing with his only daughter surfaced as he joined in Ana's make-believe world. Three minutes seemed like an eternity, but he knew he was literally and figuratively toying with the risk of getting caught. While Ana was occupied retrieving more furry friends to join the world where tall neck giraffes were doctors and long nosed elephants were scientists, Whisper pulled a burner phone from his black leather vest pocket.

Ring. Ring.

At first, the person who was receiving the blocked number call resisted answering it, but felt compelled to swipe her phone to accept the call. Once both were connected, silence screamed at the top of its lungs. It was Detective Lawson's private number so she was hesitant to speak. She was prepared to hear a late evening automated message that her car warranty was about to expire or some other irrelevant pesky nonsense.

"Little Mouse. Little Mouse. You look to the sky for me when there's chaos all around you," Whisper brazenly broke the ice.

Detective Lawson's senses pinged all over the place. Goosebumps erupted on her arms. Not only were her suspicions of a lone sniper were confirmed, but now she had the sniper's voice.

"And I guess you're the cat." She suppressed her eagerness by speaking matter-of-factly.

"Of course," Whisper said.

"What if I want to be the cat in this scenario?"

"Impossible. A cat is free from restrictions," he said like a teacher correcting his student. "Nothing has my hands tied."

"Well, nothing will stop me from getting you." Her tongue was sharp and her breathing began to elevate. "Those detectives you killed at the Brooklyn Blitz were good people. They were my friends. Damn you! Why?" Detective Lawson squeezed hard on her iPhone.

"A therapist. I'm not. At times I felt like a priest as fools confessed all of their sins or prayed to their God before I sent them home." Whisper took a moment to bask in his euphemism. "The answers you seek can be found on an expensive shrink's couch."

"Can you answer this? Are you watching me now?" Detective Lawson moved swiftly away from her bedroom window.

"Ha. Ha." Whisper found humor in her question. "That would be no fun. Our dance just started."

"I only dance with someone after getting their name." Detective Lawson was playing chess.

"You're quick on your feet, but there are only two types of people who know the name I go by—those who employ me and those who should fear me. For your sake, I'll remain anonymous." Whisper looked at his watch and then over at Ana who was still fully engaged in her fantasy world of talking stuffed animals. "Sadly, I have to cut this dance short. Tonight I did the NYPD a favor. A really bad man and some other unfortunate casualties are no longer breathing this fine city air, but a tiny female offspring will need to be cared for. I will text you the address of the neighbor I'll leave her with."

Click.

CHAPTER 22: VOICE

Buzz. Buzz.

Detective Lawson's phone vibrated to alert her that she had a new message. It was the address where Whisper said the little girl would be found. She wanted to call it in but didn't know how to explain how she got the address.

"'Tia, the sniper involved in the Brooklyn Blitz called me.' Yeah, that wouldn't go well," Kate thought.

She knew her lieutenant and lover would lose her mind if she knew a killer had called her directly. Detective Lawson not only had the voice of her sniper, but also had a potential crime scene to investigate that could bring her closer to him. She was determined not to do anything to jeopardize her efforts in getting him.

Buzz. Buzz.

Another text came through from the precinct: *Come in. Multiple homicides.*

About thirty minutes later, the crime scene had been taped off and put under NYPD protection. Detective Lawson arrived on the scene, but wasn't a part of the detective team assigned to the case. She knew she had to tread lightly and not seem too eager. She took full advantage of just being a highly skilled onlooker.

Detective Lawson scanned the crowd that had formed outside of the home. No one piqued her interest. Besides, she knew her sniper would be too smart to allow himself to be captured on camera. It was customary for the department to take pictures and do a video recording of the crowds that assembled outside of crime scenes. The newly instituted practice of doing so had increased arrests by fifteen percent.

Although she knew it was probably a waste of time, she wouldn't leave any stone unturned. She took pictures of the crowd with her personal cellphone. She quickly grew bored of crowd gazing and with a bit of luck she found herself in the same room with Ana. She couldn't resist the opportunity to ask the lone survivor and only witness to have probably seen the sniper a few questions.

"Hi, Ana, I'm Detective Lawson. Did you see the man's face who brought you to your neighbor's house?" Detective Lawson wasted no time on trying to get Ana to warm up to her.

Ana nodded.

"Is there anything you remember about him?" Detective Lawson asked.

Ana covered her tiny mouth as she yawned. Then, surprisingly, she gave a slight smile on her innocent face. "He likes to dance. I like to dance too." Ana did a twirl she had learned at her overpriced dance class.

"If this situation wasn't so bleak, this would be an adorable moment," Detective Lawson thought. "She's so cute and naïve now, but countless hours of therapy is headed her way."

A representative from Child Services introduced herself to the uniformed officer who was standing guard at the door. She flashed her badge as if to announce she was of importance. The lady looked to be in her early thirties and had a donut physique. She kneeled down the best she could next to Ana. She peered up at Detective Lawson. She made eye contact and smiled with a perfect set of bleached white teeth.

The exchange between the two made Detective Lawson a bit uncomfortable. She looked away to avoid being accused later by Lt. Marks of flirting with the agent. By the time she fixed her eyes on Ana again, the little girl was being escorted to exit the room.

"Ana, do you remember anything else?" Detective Lawson yelled across the room. "Please! Anything!"

The little girl broke free of the Child Services lady's dainty grasp. She rushed over to Detective Lawson. Ana raised her index finger to her mouth as if she wanted what she was going to say to be kept a secret. "He said to tell you his name is Whisper."

To Detective Lawson, Christmas had come early. She had a name to call the image that haunted her restless dreams. It was a gift just for her and she planned to keep it a secret for only Ana to share.

The next morning, local news outlets and Internet media sources alike ran with a story that an alleged hit man for hire had met his match. The focus was on how many unsolved homicide cases could be closed with the evidence the NYPD was confident in finding on the hit man's thumb drive discovered inside a false floorboard in the home. There was no talk about catching the murderer who had executed three people and left a little girl parentless. Instead, hungry journalists, eager readers, and many of the men and women of the NYPD wanted to expose Pedro for who he was—a bad guy.

CHAPTER 23: RUNNING

Darby had taken up running at several of the Manhattan parks. Each one boasted its own uniqueness of brilliant colors, urban backdrops, spacious greenery, and interesting food vendors. None were exempt at having a homeless person or more using the park as a home address. She varied her parks, times, and routes. Darby was unapologetic to anyone's personal space. She ran free. Her type of terrain was anywhere she wanted to put one foot in front of the other.

Although she had abandoned the fear of being seen by one of Tyrus's goons, she wore her wireless ear buds on the lowest setting. Darby was very much aware of her surroundings and concealed a small-unissued firearm in her hydration belt. Running seemed to expel some tension and helped her gain an extra hour of undisturbed sleep between her reoccurring bouts of a shotgun flash and the faces of the assholes responsible for Noah's death. All in all, insomnia was still her bedfellow.

Nevertheless, the lack of sleep didn't have any noticeable ill effects on Darby's natural beauty, nor did it cause her to lose focus on what her ultimate reason for existing was—revenge. She had only visited three of the thirty plus recognized parks in Manhattan before her appetite for running was satisfied by the many splendors of Inwood Hill Park. She had fallen in love with its bike and hiking trails. Darby found that early evening running, about two hours past the bustling end-of-work crowd, was the best time to run. The amount of causal onlookers, walkers, and runners had decreased significantly. She could run practically undisturbed.

Darby had soon become a regular figure at the park. As a result, she had become uniquely aware of subtle changes to things routinely present like faces, smells, extremely long-leashed pets, and sounds. Like a seagull impatiently hovering over shore goers waiting for food to be dropped, one stray looked forward to Darby's visits to the park. He welcomed her lightly toasted turkey bacon bagel sandwiches she left him.

After having a solid run and doing a good deed by feeding a homeless man, Darby went back to her place to shower and prepare for bed. Her tiny studio space was just what she needed. Her futon did as advertised; posed as a couch by day and bed by night. It was the only furniture in the 300 square feet living space. Darby's temporary dwelling was on a monthly lease that she acquired with an alias. The utilities were under a different name too. She went to extreme measures to minimize her footprint in the room just in case she needed to vacate without notice.

Buzz. Buzz.

"Any word?" Liam's text appeared across Darby's iPhone screen.

She intentionally didn't respond, but couldn't shake the implications behind those two words. Darby was in a constant war with the values that her parents had lovingly spoon-fed her against the tantalizing desire for revenge, but her demons seemed to always have the upper hand. "No more running from it," she thought.

It was time to clear her head of all things restricting her from doing what it would take in order to truly begin the healing process; not the lies she crafted so neatly for her head shrink. It was later in the evening, but not too late to contact her parents.

Knock knock.

Darby sent her father a coded text that meant she wanted to FaceTime. She waited for the appropriate response from him: "We're there ....."

Once he replied, the clock started ticking. The five dots meant in five minutes. Both had high anticipation of the soon-to-be meeting.

Darby initiated the FaceTime. The buffering time between the connections seemed to take longer than expected. Her father and mother were in their bedroom, joined at the shoulders to make sure they both could be seen on the screen.

"Mom. Dad. How's it going?" Darby didn't let on she had been tracking their comings and goings for weeks.

"Baby girl, what's going on?" Her father was relieved they didn't have to speak in code. He remembered that the mere fact she addressed them as her parents was the signal they could speak freely.

"Your father and I have been so worried." Her mother spoke with desperation. "You gonna cause me to drink."

"Dear, you know you don't need help pouring yourself a glass of wine," Darby's father joked.

"Ha. Ha," Darby laughed on cue.

"Don't take her side. You know this has been stressful on all of us, especially Rowan." Her mother's comments stopped the light banter.

"Is she sleeping?" Darby asked.

"No, she's in her room probably still practicing her cheer for class tomorrow," her mother gleefully said.

Darby took a deep breath before she asked, "Can I see her?"

Her parents would never deny their child her parenting rights, but they were smart enough to know inviting Rowan to the call meant they couldn't ask anything more about what was going on with their own daughter. George slid out of view of the Mac's camera. He motioned for his wife to keep talking while he went to get Rowan from the other room.

Rowan didn't give anyone a chance to prepare for her entrance. She darted into her grandparents' room the moment her Pop Pop told her that her mother wanted to speak to her.

"Mommmmy?" Rowan wasn't even breathing hard as she screamed with excitement to see her mother. "When are you coming home?"

"Wow! Look at my little baby girl getting so big." Darby kept up the pretense that she hadn't seen Rowan for a while, but always maintained a close watch on her family.

"Look, Mommy. Do you want to see me cheer?" Rowan took complete control of the angle of the camera.

"Of course I do. Let me see what my baby is working with." Darby knew the entire routine thanks to a tiny spy camera she had hidden in her parents' family room.

Rowan was bubbling with extra excitement. Darby hoped she'd start with the counting cheer because that was her favorite. Rowan didn't disappoint.

"One, two, we can see right through … you." Rowan swiped two small fingers across her eyes. "Three, four, our team is so much better than …yours," she said with a scowl of conceit on her face.

That look was Darby's favorite. She knew her daughter didn't know the first thing about being a snob, but that face said it all. Without caring if they realized she was watching them all along, Darby stood up and finished the cheer with her daughter. She had the words and movements down to perfection.

Darby and Rowan continued performing the counting cheer together. "Five, six, you'll continue to miss." Mom and daughter pretended to take an exaggerated awkward basketball shot. "Seven, eight, oops, it's too late. Nine, ten, our team wins again!"

They repeated that cheer over and over again. Darby enjoyed her time with her daughter. She knew she could just relocate and live happily ever after, but they had taken her only child's father away and for that happily ever after would have to wait.

CHAPTER 24: BACON BAGEL

The next day, Darby met up with Liam and Indigo. It had been several days since their last interaction. Darby had arranged for the meeting place to be just outside of Inwood Hill Park.

Liam and Indigo sat quietly in their rental SUV. They were still awkwardly trying to get passed the kiss that happened between them. Liam wanted to finally move forward with his feelings and Indigo would've been accepting, but he insisted she'd go back home. Leaving her friend alone to handle something that seemed potentially dangerous wasn't an option for her.

Darby waved them over to where she was standing. She watched them exit the car. Liam's arms had muscles on top of muscles and his strange friend had clearly changed her appearance from the last time they had met. It was the blue baseball hat that Indigo was wearing that Darby took as a sign that she was doing the right thing.

"Still here I see," Darby said without expecting a response.

"Going for a run?" Liam scratched his head at how Darby was dressed.

"Something like that." Darby took in a much-needed breath before going on to tell them who had murdered Noah. "Tyrus and his crew are responsible for Noah's death."

"No. No. No." Liam shook his head in disbelief. "Impossible."

"I saw him with my own eyes," Darby said with some bite to her tone.

Crunch! Crunch!

Liam pounded his fists into a nearby tree. He hit the large indigenous tree with disregard to his own wellbeing. Although his hands had been conditioned to be the perfect weapons for fighting, it wasn't too long before blood oozed from areas of ripped skin.

"Who is Tyrus?" Indigo wrote. She wanted to be clued-in.

"Noah's damn brother!" Liam yelled as he slouched down under the same tree he was just trying to punch a hole through. "Tell me it was someone else." Liam was prepared to finally hear who

73

Noah's murderer was, but never in a million years had he expected it would've been his own brother. "The asshole will die twice."

"What?" Indigo still felt like she was outside looking in on what was happening.

Darby explained to Indigo how Tyrus had faked his death to avoid getting himself killed by a major drug trafficker that he had double-crossed. And how he had manipulated Noah into his plot to take over the drug and gun scene by eliminating his threatening competition while stepping out of the ominous shadow of his brother.

"Jealous bastard!" Her words were a bit smeared because she'd pressed down hard as she wrote.

Indigo was up to speed and just as angry too. Family meant the world to her, so Tyrus had committed the ultimate sin.

"By the way," Darby tugged at Indigo's symbolic blue hat, "hair or no hair, you're still sexy. I know you're turning heads."

"Right," Liam confirmed what many people had told Indigo most of her life.

Ha. Ha. Ha. Just like that, the tension was broken. Darby and Liam laughed as if they just heard the funniest joke ever. Although very humble, even Indigo smiled and was in better spirits.

"May I get a—" Darby began and was cut short by the counter person vendor truck at the park, who recognized a regular customer.

"Egg, turkey, cheese, and bacon bagel. Lightly toasted," the counter person said with rehearsed accuracy. "Correct?"

"Absolutely," Darby smiled.

Liam and Indigo looked puzzled. Darby had texted them earlier that it was go-time. But she was dressed like she was going for a run and ordering a breakfast sandwich in the early evening.

"What are you doing?" Indigo wrote what Liam was thinking too.

"Buying someone his last meal on earth," Darby said without any reservation.

CHAPTER 25: SHOCK TREATMENT

The park had thinned out and there was about an hour left before darkness took over the skyline. Those that remained were the regulars who stayed in their own space throughout the park. Darby's plan was simple. She was going to drop the sandwich deeper into the thickest wooded area of the park. Then they were to hide and wait until her unexpected stray grabbed the bag. Her last part of the plan was airtight. Basically, once they surrounded their victim, she tapped her pouch on her hydration belt and said, "He doesn't get to finish the sandwich."

Armani Trio watched Darby place the bag on a nearby bench. His clothes were worn to say the least. He had a hitch in his walk. They weren't sure if he was injured or it was due to wearing two different pairs of sneakers on his feet. To him Darby had proven over time that she was safe, a person who came bearing delicious treats. She hadn't even run out of sight before he raced towards the bench. He folded the bag over his lap as if he didn't want to spill food on his already grimy pants.

"How's the sandwich?" Liam calmly said.

Armani waved Liam on his way without taking his attention away from the bacon that hung freely from a bite he had just taken.

"My friend, what's your name?" Liam tried again to get the man's attention.

"Armani Trio. But my friends call me Trio." He spoke with a mouth full of chewed food. "You can call me Armani." Armani took large bites as if he needed to finish the sandwich before someone came along to take it from him.

"Do you remember me?' Darby walked up to see Liam and Indigo standing around a man who was just about done eating the bagel.

Smack!

Darby knocked the last bit of the sandwich out of his hand. She wasn't about to let him finish it.

Armani crabbed crawled to salvage what was left. He tried cramming what he could into his mouth dirt and remains from the bagel.

"I said, do you remember me?" Darby stepped on a quarter-sized piece of bacon that remained on the ground.

Armani lifted his head to see the person who insisted on getting his attention. "Yes, I know. You the lady who leaves me food in the park." Armani was agitated. "If you wanted a thank you—thank you. Now, could you lift your foot? There's some bacon with my name on it."

"Here's a name for you. Noah!" Darby spoke through clenched teeth.

Something imploded inside the filthy man. He sobbed with uncontrolled body twitches. He stood up, forgetting all about the last piece of bacon. He cried out with half-chewed food still in his mouth. "I … I … I didn't know they were gonna kill him. Noah was good to me." Armani was apologetic.

"Did you just say he was good to you?" Darby retrieved her gun from her hydration belt. She pointed the small revolver at his face.

"You must believe me. I didn't want to hurt Noah," Armani groveled. "He was always good to me."

"Tell him when you see him," Darby said as she prepared to pull the trigger.

"Wait!" Liam rushed over and lowered Darby's hand. "You said there were others. He could lead us to them."

"He's useless. I know where to find the person who could take us right to Tyrus." Darby was growing impatient.

"Are you sure this pathetic thing was directly responsible for Noah's death?" Liam sought some reassurance from Darby.

"He was there and that's all I need to say." Darby held to her conviction.

Ironically, it was Indigo who ultimately got at the truth. She was the least vested in getting revenge for Noah, but after years in therapy she noticed something familiar about Armani. Indigo was used to being a ghost during group discussions. So she easily managed to get behind Armani and put him in a chokehold.

"What are you doing? Please let me go," Armani pleaded.

Indigo tightened her hold to restrict his breathing.

"That'll take too long. Move out of the way!" Darby demanded.

Indigo had her hands too full to write that she knew what she was doing, so she gave Darby a look that said she was in control.

Armani was frightened for his life and weak. He gave up his control of the others in his head before Indigo could truly bring the pain.

"Young lady, this is barbaric," the professor struggled to speak clearly. "Take your arms from around my neck. This isn't how you greet people."

Hearing a different voice come from the same filthy man that Indigo had her arms locked around his head and neck baffled both Darby and Liam. Indigo loosened her grip, but wasn't ready to completely allow him to be set free. She was pleased to know that her suspicions were right and that Armani behaved like he had inner demons that he struggled with—all of which, had separate personalities.

"Please, let me go so we can talk about this like civilized people. I can assure you that Trio had nothing to do with Noah's death. The poor boy wouldn't hurt a nagging mosquito," the professor spoke with confidence.

"And you?" Darby questioned.

"No, child. These hands are for experimenting and inventing. Now tell the she hulk to let me loose," the professor pleaded again.

Darby and Indigo were speaking the same nonverbal body language. Darby nodded and on cue Indigo reapplied her stranglehold around the filthy man's neck. The professor gave more of a fight, but each time he struggled the hold got tighter.

"Let me go. NOW!" Tell-it-First spoke with his usual lisp. "I'm gonna stomp your foot."

His slow, telegraphed attempt to stamp on Indigo's foot failed miserably. But she did loosen her grip to allow him to speak some more.

"What you looking at?" Tell-it-First directed his aggression towards Liam. "I'll punch you in the face."

"Did you say my lace?" Liam found humor with the filthy man's idle threat.

"I said face, big man. You lucky she's holding me back." Tell-it-First swiped at Liam and again missed horribly.

Indigo didn't need a signal from anyone to reapply her chokehold. She didn't mind instituting shock therapy to Armani, but was growing tired of his many personalities. She hoped they'd get the right one sooner than later.

Tell-it-First struggled in his uncoordinated way, but Grandma was the ultimate protector for the cast of misfits. She took the reins and wasn't about to give them back.

"So, they keep Grandma buried, but now they call on me in a hurry." Grandma moved purposely and seemed unworried of the chokehold. "Spanish vixen, unless we about to do some kind of new tango, let …go. You wanted me. Here's …Grandma!"

Liam motioned for Indigo to release her hold and to make her way back over to him. He was taken back by what he was seeing and hearing. A cowering filthy man was now moving and speaking like a confident elderly woman and one of his eyes went from blue to evergreen.

"That's … who … was … there," Darby said as she tried catching her breath.

Hearing Grandma's voice and seeing her mannerisms sent Darby into an involuntary panic attack. The weeks of therapy didn't prepare her for facing one of Noah's tormentors for the first time. She fell down to both knees and the gun dropped to the ground as she grabbed for her chest. Visions of Noah collapsing in Tyrus's arms and the shotgun blast kept her immobilized.

"You." Grandma directed her attention towards Darby. "Leaving those tasteless bagels. Asshole. Just adding salt and pepper ain't seasoning."

Late September still had an unusual steaming hot feel, but Armani wore a tattered heavy winter coat. Grandma graciously removed the coat like it was worth thousands of dollars. She folded it neatly before laying it carefully on the nearby bench. Then she twisted a piece of the back part of the putrid Nike t-shirt she was wearing.

"So, who do I kill first? Baby Hercules, Spanish vixen, or the one on her knees?" Eyeing Darby she said, "Yeah, I'll torture you the worst."

"You talk too much." Liam had heard enough.

Ready to make quick work of Grandma, he rushed towards her, but was met with a vicious flying knee that just about took his nose off his face. He collapsed to the ground, seeing stars. Grandma leaped at him with the intent to drive her knee into his throat, but Indigo tackled her in midair. The two of them scrambled quickly back to their feet.

"Seems like the cat has your tongue, but I plan to have some fun." Grandma was feeling herself.

Grandma stood in a fighting stance and, like the iconic Bruce Lee, waved her hand inviting Indigo to come fight her. However, Grandma didn't wait for Indigo to strike first. Instead, she charged Indigo with a superman punch that was just a distraction for her deadly rear round house kick to the head.

Indigo managed to block the punch and narrowly escaped the kick to her head. Her hat went flying off her head as the brim of it got the brunt of the force from the kick. Indigo's arm was already bruising from blocking the punch. She couldn't believe how fast and strong her opponent was, especially with a name like Grandma. Indigo knew she had her hands full, but her spirits wouldn't be broken.

"You ... too sexy for that hat. Too sexy like that." Grandma was in her glory.

Liam was trying to shake off the cobwebs. He couldn't stand without losing his balance and falling back to the ground. Darby was just a spectator to the panic attack that consumed her tensed body. She closed her eyes and attempted to do her deep breathing exercises, but haunting images of Noah's limped body sucked her the breath and any hope of her regaining her composure.

Grandma and Indigo continued to exchange punches, kicks, leg-swipes, and the occasional head bunts. Grandma was getting the better of Indigo. She seemed to be getting stronger as the fight went on.

Indigo's physical state of being was fading fast. Her pride kept her from running over to grab Darby's gun. She was determined to shut Grandma up for good or die trying. Indigo had several prominent bruises on her arms and legs. Blood escaped from various parts of her body, but none was worse than the cut above her right eye. It wasn't a deep cut, but the blood blurred her vision in that eye.

Grandma strategically moved and attacked Indigo's right side. It was a well-placed kick to Indigo's stomach that brought the silent warrior to her knees. Grandma pounced quickly by scrambling behind Indigo to apply her own suffocating chokehold. Indigo had no gas left in the tank to fight out of Grandma's vice grip. Grandma used her body weight to take Indigo down to the ground and scissor locked her legs around the helpless Spanish vixen.

"Go to sleep, my pretty." Grandma licked Indigo's head. "I will wake you when I'm ready to eat."

Indigo's body was going limp.

Boom!

Liam surprised Grandma with a thunderous hammer fist to the face. "I told you, you talk too much." His second hammer fist caused a large lump to appear on Grandma's forehead.

Grandma might've been a skilled ferocious killer, but she still had Armani's 150-pound physique. For most people she was an unstoppable predator, but was no match for an angry and highly skilled fighter like Liam. He pulled Grandma up from the ground by her filthy hair. She attempted a knee to his groin, but Liam blocked it with his own knee. He wasn't going to underestimate her again.

A battered Indigo tried standing. She managed to get to her feet, but bent over in exhaustion and pain. She spat blood on the ground.

Seeing his friend beaten up drove Liam crazily insane. He pounded on Grandma with deadly force. He kneed her to the face and slammed her head first to the ground. Although he admired her guts and lack of fear, he was ready to end her life.

"Stop! NYPD!" Detective Lawson yelled as she drew her gun.

CHAPTER 26: JUDGMENT

Grandma was too injured to resist Armani taking charge again of the group. He was the weakest of all personalities, but the one who saw the opportunity to save himself from Liam.

"Please help me!" Armani begged as he slowly got back to his feet. "They're trying to kill me."

Detective Lawson surveyed the group. She recognized Liam as the recent heavy weight champion of the UFC and the gorgeous Indigo who always stole camera time as one of Liam's corner people. "What are they doing here?" she thought. However, her main interest was on FBI Agent Darby Rice.

Bang! Bang!

Detective Lawson fired two shots. Her bullets went in separate directions. One hit Armani's shoulder blade while the other chipped off a piece of the back of his head. He was dead by the time his body hit the ground.

"Ma'am, it looks like he attacked you." Detective Lawson directed her statement towards Indigo.

Liam and Indigo were shell-shocked. But Darby, who was finally freed from her anxiety by the sounds of the gunfire, wasn't surprised to see the detective.

"I thought I'd lost you," Darby spoke directly to Detective Lawson.

"Huh." Detective Lawson was a bit surprised that Darby knew she was being tailed. "You did. This is a big park. I've been looking for you for the last twenty minutes."

"Now what?" Darby was bothered by the interruption, but more disappointed with how she'd reacted to Grandma.

"Let's join forces," Detective Lawson said.

"We're good," Darby said, without giving the request a chance.

"You didn't look good from my view. Look, I'm not here to judge. I just think with your Bureau training and connections," Detective Lawson tried pleading her case.

"Bureau, like FBI? Darby, are you an agent?" Liam needed an answer.

Liam and Indigo were more confused about what they had just heard.

To not be outdone, Darby revealed what she knew. "Listen, detective. Wait, I mean, Kate Lawson, just because you know who employs me, doesn't mean we need your help."

"If you know me, then you must know I am the lone officer who survived the Brooklyn Blitz." Detective Lawson wasn't prepared to accept no as an answer.

"Congratulations. No." Darby still wasn't accepting new recruits on the team. She walked over to Liam, who had been caring for Indigo. "Let's go."

"The sniper is still alive. He contacted me and I got his street name. We are in this together, regardless if we work together or not." Detective Lawson played her best hand.

"This isn't sanctioned," Darby sighed.

"I know. I owe someone my life," Detective Lawson said.

"Name?" Darby questioned.

"He goes by the name of Whisper," Detective Lawson explained.

"Any hits?" Darby hoped for the best.

"No, but I'm still digging," Detective Lawson said.

"I'll be in touch. Right now, you have a body to tend to." Darby helped Liam do a two-person arm carry for the injured Indigo.

"Wait. She'll need to make a statement. Besides, she needs medical help." Detective Lawson appealed for some assistance.

"Kate, she'll be recognized. Remember, this must be off the record. Let's see what you bring to the team. You got it. Right?" Darby smirked. "Don't worry. If you can't, I won't judge you."

Police car sirens were heard in the near distance.

CHAPTER 27: REGROUP

Indigo was sprawled out on the back seat. She had aches and pains in places she didn't know were possible. She had stopped spitting up blood by the time they made it back to the car. She knew that was a good sign that she probably didn't have any internal injuries. Indigo didn't want to visit the emergency room and be the reason their mission failed. She knew her current physical condition was probably causing Liam and Darby some doubt. Without one grunt or ow, she mustered up enough strength to sit up and fasten her seatbelt like her bruises had already mended.

Liam drove, but was driving on autopilot. He felt the one to blame for his dearest friend's injuries. He had stopped Darby from shooting Armani when she first had the chance and he underestimated the skill set of Grandma. He didn't want Indigo to stay, but now that she was there, it was his job to protect her. But he believed he'd failed Indigo, Darby, and the one he'd once called a brother—Noah. Liam looked in the rearview mirror and caught a quick glimpse of Indigo grimace in pain. "She could've been killed because of me," he thought.

On the other hand, Darby thought the silence in the SUV was due to her hiding her status as an FBI agent. She knew telling Liam would've complicated things. She felt he would've tried stopping her from getting her revenge. Then she considered the silence was due to them being embarrassed for her because she fell apart like a soggy piece of bread. That angered her more and before she knew it, she was speaking her mind without any reservations.

"Liam, you weren't there. Noah sacrificed his good life, fame, and money to see his brother's killers were dealt with. But in the end, it was his own sorry ass brother that set him up. Damn coward!" Darby didn't care to take a breath. "Yeah, I'm an agent, but I'm not following protocol. And don't give me the 'what would Noah want me to do' speech. I want them dead. That's it!"

Darby found herself breathing hard, like she had just climbed seven flights of steps. She waited for Liam to speak, but was surprised it was Indigo who spoke up first.

"Give me a few hours ..." Indigo labored heavily as she retrieved her notepad and pencil. *"I'll be ready."*

Liam and Darby knew better. Indigo would need a week or two before she would be at her best again. Darby couldn't understand how a complete stranger was all in for a man she had never met. Liam was still committed to see the mission through for his fallen brother, but the stakes had just hit an all-time high when they hurt Indigo.

Tears broke free from the pond that had swelled up in Liam's eyes. "No mercy."

Darby was relieved to hear that her core group was still intact, but knew the tougher challenge was just ahead. She had discovered Big 60's most frequently visited places, but hadn't seen him for a couple of days. She was good with his sudden disappearance because it would allow time for Indigo to heal and for her to search her databases for what she could collect on the sniper named Whisper.

"My silent warrior, you have my respect in more ways than one," Darby thought.

CHAPTER 28: TURN IT DOWN

It was about ten in the evening by the time Kate was able to leave the precinct. She wasted no time getting to her jeep. As she drove home, she questioned herself if she was consistent in telling her story in the statement she submitted for record. She knew firsthand that those who were hiding the truth would trip up on what they said versus what they put in writing.

She had typed up her statement and was asked too many direct and indirect questions concerning the shooting of the homeless man in the park. The gun she had used to kill him was one she'd acquired from the streets. It was a throwaway Glock 43 she had planned to use on Whisper. Kate didn't have a chance to ditch it, so she concealed it back in her ankle holster. Carrying a gun was second nature to her, but carrying the murder weapon into a police department made her feel exposed.

The gun seemed to generate extreme heat and made her ankle feel like it was on fire. "Calm your nerves. Don't flake out now," Kate tried coaching herself off the panic bridge. "Your ankle is fine."

Detective Lawson kept to her story that while she was running in the park she heard two gunshots. By the time she made it over to where the sounds had come from, she saw someone running from the murder scene. She said she couldn't get a clear description of the runner. Kate added that she wasn't even sure if the runner had a gun or not. She wanted her statement to be so vague that she wouldn't be asked in the future to be a potential witness.

An incoming call from Tia freed her from her thoughts.

Kate's jeep alerted her that she was receiving a call from Tia. She accepted the call just before Tia was sent to her voice message.

"Hello," Kate tried to stay calm.

"Why am I just hearing about you being in an area where someone was gunned down?" Tia skipped over the typical greeting.

"I wouldn't say a homeless man being killed in a park fits the description of being gunned down." Kate didn't want her lieutenant to employ more resources than were necessary to investigate the murder.

"There you go, downplaying things. You could've been in danger." Tia was speaking from her heart.

"I'm not. I ran over to see if I could help. It's our job, right?" Kate said, with a bit of sarcasm.

"I'm getting dressed as we speak and I'll meet you at your place," Tia stated.

"No, it's late. I just want to shower and call it a night. Besides, I won't be good bedside company tonight." Kate sounded exhausted.

"There you go, pushing me away again. I just want to make sure you're okay and I'll be there in the morning to help you sort anything new that comes to mind," Tia pleaded her case.

"I appreciate you, but please know I'm not trying to push you away. I just want to clean up and sleep the rest of this night away. I promise I'll call you first thing in the morning to discuss any dreams I might have," Kate responded.

Click.

The signal was lost between the two as Kate pulled into her underground parking garage. She typically parked on the street, but after circling the block once she decided to take advantage of the monthly $300 dollar bill she paid for indoor parking. She figured Tia would call her back, but that call didn't come. Kate hoped Tia remembered about the dead spot and didn't feel like she had hung up on her. In either case, Kate planned to clear up things in the morning.

It was only a matter of minutes after stepping foot in her home when she heard a knock at her door.

"Tia, you're so damn stubborn." Kate walked over to unlock the door. "Why didn't you use your key?"

Kate was surprised to see the three people standing on the opposite side of her door.

"May we come in?" Darby asked as she stepped by Kate. "Nice place."

Indigo and Liam waited to be formally allowed into Kate's home.

"Come in. Make yourself comfortable. Clearly, she has," Kate said, slightly biting her bottom lip.

"Why are you still wearing the same clothes from earlier today?" Darby spoke but didn't make eye contact as she observed the contents in the room.

"I was left alone to clean up things. You know ... a dead body." Kate was agitated, but managed to keep her cool.

"So, did you?" Darby pushed for an answer.

"It appears that way. But time will tell." Kate wanted to fix whatever was broken between the two of them. "Hey, I don't know why I'm giving you the wrong vibe. I'm sorry I followed you. I should've approached you directly, but trust me, I just want to be a part of the team. We have the same agenda."

"You're on the team. That's why we're here." Darby explained why they were there but never acknowledged Kate's statement. "Indigo needs medical care."

"How can I help?" Kate said, eager to start contributing more to the team.

"She needs to be examined and treated, but not at a hospital. It has to be done discretely. She needs to stay here for a few days."

"What?" Indigo was a lit firecracker. She wrote with fierce strokes. *"No way!"*

"Yes, freaking way. We need to take them on at full strength. That means we need you to heal," a frustrated Liam demanded.

"Wait. She doesn't talk?" Kate asked.

"She hears perfectly so watch what you say," Darby answered. Indigo sighed hard as she raised her hands and head to the ceiling in displeasure. She knew Liam's mind was made up because he almost cussed. Indigo and Liam stared deeply into each other's eyes. It was evident that it wasn't a game of who blinks first but more of a message that they both loved the other with their life, but didn't want to fight about it Liam won in the end.

Kate snapped her fingers in between the two of them. "I want to be part of the team, but she can't stay here."

Six sets of eyes stared at Kate. The room was quiet except for her enhanced heart rate. Kate felt like she was in her own interrogation room, but this time, she was the one being accused of something. She began to ramble.

"I will do anything else, but this won't work. Besides, it's not like I have a doctor on retainer who won't question her injuries. Come

87

on, guys. There has to be another way to prove my worth to the team," Kate rationalized.

"You seem resourceful. You found me. What's really going on?" Darby questioned.

Kate paced the floor before spilling her true fear. "Right now, my girlfriend and I aren't in a good place. She doesn't know what I'm up. And she wouldn't be cool with Ms. Bombshell over here sleeping at my place."

Darby chuckled as she spoke. "You telling me you can't talk your way out of this? Just tell her your cousin came for a visit."

"Oh yeah. That's original. She'll believe this can't keep a tanned White girl has a Spanish bloodline too." Kate grabbed Darby's arm. "Listen. My girlfriend is African American and we're in a bad place right now. She's not going to wait to hear any explanation. Come on! You know this."

"Oh, cause I'm Black you want me to validate your concerns and be understanding?" Darby was enjoying Kate's predicament.

"No, I don't need validation. I just need you to know how she was the last time she was here." Kate added hand gestures as she spoke. "She was moving her head and hands like this as if she basically was on the verge of handing me my own ass."

"Girl, you right. You're in trouble." Darby smiled. Then she addressed Liam. "Let's go back to get my car."

"Wait. My girlfriend is my lieutenant at the precinct." Kate lowered her head. "This could be a problem for us all."

"Wow! When you do it, you go right to the top." Darby closed the distance between her and Kate. She whispered into Kate's ear, "We need you. Show us why you made detective."

Liam and Darby left Kate's place without saying another word. Kate pushed the door closed. She pressed her forehead against it before turning to face her injured guest.

"Do you think you can turn it down some?" Kate said.

Her statement confused Indigo. She frowned and wrote, *"What?"*

"Duh. Your looks!" Kate was seriously joking.

Indigo concealed her smile as she motioned for Kate to tell her where she could rest her head for the night.

"Down the hall on the left," Kate said in between her own rant. "Like, who gets bloodied up in a fight and still looks like a sexy model? Hey, don't go yet. We need to get our story straight."

Indigo didn't break stride as she reached the bedroom she'd call home for the next few days.

Kate yelled, "My girlfriend is not going to take pity on you because you don't talk! Whisper, if you got the shot, take it now. You'll be doing me a favor. Uh!"

CHAPTER 29: TRUST ME

Tyrus ordered Big 60 to take Rip and Cord to collect money owed from a gun smuggler out of Baltimore. The whole thing didn't make sense to Big 60, but he knew his insubordination back at the safe house would have consequences. He was instructed to take Rip and Cord to a location about ten miles from Baltimore's inner harbor area. He was given specific instructions to wait in the car for them to return with the payment owed.

It was just past seven in the evening. The sun had just set about forty minutes earlier, but darkness wasn't yet a smothering blanket over the city. Big 60 had the car running but the headlights were out. The inside of the car illuminated the green light from the radio and the car's plush dashboard. The car wasn't stolen, but was registered to one of Tyrus's ghost fleets that led to dead ends about who actually owned it.

Although Big 60 was as hardcore as they came, he couldn't shake the special feelings he had developed for his two mentees. He wanted to pull off to keep them from any potential danger, but his loyalty to Tyrus ran too deep in his veins to overcome the intoxication of devotion to a person who he consistently sought after for approval.

"Don't come back unless you have the money," Big 60 barked the same line that was fed to him by Tyrus.

Rip and Cord exited the vehicle. Cord sat in the passenger seat, and imitated a valet by rushing to the door behind him. He opened the door for his friend Mel, who had finally freed himself from the seatbelt and bounced out of the car.

Mel fist bumped Cord and said, "Let's get this money."

Rip and Big 60 watched Cord interact with his imaginary friend, who was larger than life in his complex, misfiring mind.

"Careful, guys." Big 60 waited until they were out of earshot to speak again. He watched them get closer to what looked to be a two-story home. He knew it was a death trap and that Rip and Cord had very little chance of returning alive. A sudden rush that a father would have for his kids came over him. He turned the car off. He squeezed the door latch and opened it a few centimeters. Big 60 stopped just before the dome light inside the car was activated. He slammed the door closed. "Dammit!"

Rip had her suspicions that the two of them were sure to end up on the losing side of this mission. Yet she was relieved somehow that Big 60 wasn't in on the setup. That feeling drove her even more to prove to him that they were worthy of how he cared for them. As she approached the foreboding building, she remembered what she had first told Big 60: "I'm ready for my life to change."

Cord and Mel followed behind Rip. They had a secret crush on the woman that had openly accepted them both. Well, Mel was more open with his feelings but respected the only woman who seemed to give him life and existence like Cord. They agreed to protect her with their being. Rip might have led the way, but once they reached the corner of the home, Cord was bent on taking the lead.

"Shh. Let Mel take a look before we go in," Cord whispered to Rip.

Rip didn't appear to show any lack of faith of Mel truly existing. She simply nodded and waited for Cord to tell her when it was time to enter the building.

Cord closed his eyes and waited for Mel to return with vital information that detailed where the dangers were throughout the shady-looking home. Mel returned after what seemed to be a few minutes or more with the layout of the building and where the gunmen waited in hiding. He quickly shared what he saw with Cord, whose eyes grew as big as bowling balls as he listened to the details.

"They must've seen us coming. Because they are armed and hiding in the shadows waiting for us," Cord shared with Rip.

Rip's suspicions were confirmed. She glanced back at Big 60 who was still waiting in the car for them to return. Rip was more comfortable wielding her knives, but wasn't foolish enough to only bring knives to a gunfight.

"We have a plan," Cord bubbled with excitement. "You trust us, right?"

Rip nodded again.

"Wait for my signal. Then go in." Cord ran towards the other side of the house.

"What's the signal?" Rip whispered as Cord clumsily took off running.

"What are they doing?" Big 60 thought their hesitation meant they were scared. "Don't go out like damn cowards. Be fearless." He slammed his hands hard on the steering wheel and, for a moment, rested his forehead on it. When he looked up again, Cord looked as if he was running away. "What the hell!"

Big 60 retrieved his Glock from the hidden compartment under his floor mat. He swung open his car door. It boomeranged hard right back towards him. He stopped it from slamming shut, but didn't take a step out. He sat for a moment as his animalistic instincts of fight, no matter the odds, battled against the instinct of a parent wanting to see his kids grow up to complete a task.

Bang! Bang! Bang!

He closed his car door again when he heard the sound of someone emptying a gun clip and spaced-out return fire.

"I guess that's the signal," Rip thought.

Rip rushed in, expecting utter chaos, but oddly, there was no time for a sense of clarity. The windows were naked of curtains and blinds, so there was light dancing in from the September skies. She saw several bodies sprawled all across the floor. They weren't clumped together. Instead, they were lying next to the makeshift shield they had apparently thought would've kept them safe.

She couldn't believe what she was seeing. There were barriers created out of a tattered mattress, an extremely faded cherry wood coffee table, and a love seat that appeared to have no more love to give. As she stepped deeper into the room, she noticed patterned bullet sized holes in the creaky floor. Those barriers might have had a chance to protect those in hiding, but weren't a match for the cunningness of Cord. He'd managed to enter the shallow basement of the shabby house to shoot upwards through the dirty, peeling linoleum floor.

Shoop! Shoop!

The muffled gun blast from Cord's silencer was just audible enough to shake Rip back to the present. He had made quick work of one of the bodies that still had some life left. He gave Rip the universal sign to be quiet as he pointed towards the steps.

"Mel said there are more hiding upstairs. Stay behind me," Cord whispered with complete confidence.

Shoop!

Rip shot one of the fallen neighborhood thugs who had Cord in his sights. His gun fell from his hands and made a hard thud sound on the floor. Rip and Cord prepared for an ambush to come from the top floor, but no one descended from the steps.

Tyrus, who was big on watching mob and old martial arts movies, lived for the dramatics. Like the movie *Game of Death* where the iconic Bruce Lee had to fight for his life through different levels to overcome his tormentors, he had instructed his hired gunmen to only attack once Rip and Cord made it to their level of the two-story home. Tyrus made it clear that nothing good would come of those who didn't obey that order.

Big 60 hated the fact that he didn't know what was happening. He figured if he heard the sounds of gunfire, his two disciples were still alive. Each second of silence felt like his heart was going to burst through his chest.

Cord led the charge up to the second level. He and Rip slowly moved through the area, hitting their moving targets with precision. They covered each other's backs while inexperienced gunmen shot in many directions but straight. Rip and Cord replaced empty clips as they cleared each room on the second floor. They weren't going to stop until the money they had come for was in their possession.

"Please don't shoot! You can have the money," a tiny voice was heard from behind the last door.

Rip cautiously pushed opened the door. Cord readied his gun for whoever was waiting for them behind it. They were shocked to see a kid who looked to be no more than thirteen years' old standing next to a school backpack with an image of a Ninja on the outside of it.

"He's just a kid," Cord said as he kicked away a gun that was lying on the floor. "Is the money in the bag?"

"Yes. Yes. You can have it all." The boy tossed the bag towards Cord's feet and then raised his hands back in a surrendering position.

Cord placed his gun in his waistband. Then he checked the contents of the bag. There had to be at least ten thousand dollars in it.

"We got what we came for," Cord said to Rip, who was still pointing her gun at the boy. "Let's go. He's just a kid."

Rip slowly lowered her gun, but her eyes didn't stop surveying the room. The boy felt some relief, but feared for his life, so he kept his hands raised high above his head.

"Do you promise to go straight home and stay out of trouble?" Rip asked with a hint of sarcasm.

The boy nodded so hard he looked like an oversized bobble head figure. Mel paced the floor as he began to worry about Rip.

Rip stowed away her gun in the waistband of her pants. She walked towards the frightened boy. "They made you come here, didn't they?" She kept walking and didn't care to hear answers from him. "They forced that gun into your hand, right?"

"Something is wrong. Stop her!" Mel pleaded with Cord.

The blade from her knife sliced a fatal smile under the boy's chin. Rip got splattered with blood from the dying boy. She stood over him as he squirmed on the floor, gasping for air. Seeing rope, hand ties, and what appeared to be gags waiting patiently for their purpose in the corner of the room had brought back bad memories to the surface.

CHAPTER 30: VANTAGE POINT

"I was hoping for the best, but didn't really know what to expect." Big 60 was overjoyed to see the two people he actually considered more than friends return unharmed. He even welcomed Mel back to the car. "Wow! The three of you are bad asses!"

Cord held the car door open for Mel to climb in the back seat. He threw the backpack in and then slowly took a seat next to it. He knew he had ended the lives of many men that night, but the image of the terrified boy tugged hard at his conscious.

Rip opened the passenger door and graciously took a seat. She seemed so relaxed. It was as if she had just taken a walk in the park and was still relishing in the serenity of it all. "Tell your boss the job is done." Her voice was even and her words made a clear statement to Big 60.

"Yeah. I better do that," Big 60 said without letting on that Rip didn't acknowledge Tyrus as her boss.

Welcome to the family. Even split.

A text flashed across Big 60's phone screen before he got the chance to type his first word. He didn't let on that Tyrus was watching them.

"He said the money is yours to split and you are officially welcome to the family," Big 60 uttered as he started the car.

"We in the money." Mel was excited. "I know what I'm doing with my piece of the pie. Whatever I want. Ha. Ha."

Rip and Cord didn't say a word.

Whisper slowly and carefully began to dismantle his high-powered sniper rifle. He witnessed the entire pursuit of Rip and Cord as they moved through the house to capture the bag of money. He admired the moxie of Rip. Her killer instinct, which to him meant a fearlessness and willingness to do whatever it took to get the job done, was an attractive character trait.

He had been contracted by Tyrus to remove the two weeds if Big 60 tried to help them or if they attempted to run away from the job. Whisper had acquired a vantage point where he wouldn't be detected, but could see through the windows of the house as well as spy on Big 60's whereabouts. He was also given specific orders to end the lives of Rip and Cord the moment Big 60 stepped a single foot outside of his car. In big fashion, Tyrus wanted to make a grand statement that he was the boss.

As he watched Big 60 drive off, he felt a vibration in his pocket. He pulled his phone out to see the alert that money had been deposited in his offshore account. Whisper stuffed his smartphone back into his pocket, but felt empty that he didn't have his family to go home to. It was starting to be a recurring theme that he regretted choosing his life of crime and death over a normal life with his daughter and her mother.

CHAPTER 31: BREAKFAST TALK

Liam and Darby had agreed to meet at a local diner for breakfast and to discuss the next steps. He arrived first and requested a booth that was the farthest from earshot of others and the front door. Liam was punctual, but didn't mind Darby's tardiness of being almost thirty minutes late.

Darby took her seat across from Liam. Her back was to the door. She looked like she had taken special care with her appearance. Darby's hair, clothes, and makeup were flawless. Liam saw her softness and beauty that his best friend Noah had once seen.

"You're looking fancy today," Liam said as he took another sip from his second cup of coffee.

"I'm going fishing." Darby didn't bat an eye. "I've had a big one on the hook for quite some time. Now it's time to reel him in."

"I'm sure that makes sense to you. But for me, I guess my coffee hasn't kicked in yet." Liam took another swig of it.

A thin, wiry waitress with large framed glasses came over to their table. She took both of their food orders, but couldn't stop staring at Liam. She recognized him but couldn't figure out where. Her curiosity got the better of her.

"Are you famous or something?" the waitress directed her question towards Liam.

He was quick to respond with a witty remark. "Yes, just ask my mother."

"Ha. Ha." The waitress and Liam laughed, but Darby kept her game face on.

"I'll be back as soon as your food is up." The waitress walked off to submit their order to the cooking station.

Liam changed expressions quickly as he redirected his attention back to Darby. "Don't let that scowl on your face become permanent."

"If you're having second thoughts, I'll get it done by myself." Darby meant it.

"No second thoughts. Indigo is laid up, trying to heal from her injuries. I'm in it to the end. But I don't have any kids. Let me take it from here," Liam said with sincerity.

"The kid card isn't a part of my fifty-two-card deck. Tyrus will pay for what he did to Noah." Darby's breathing began to get heavy. "You weren't there when … when Noah hugged his brother like a loving mother does her child. Then to see his body jerk and that horrified look Noah had as he realized his brother had betrayed him." She paused for a moment to regain normal breathing. "The hurt Noah must've felt to know he had a brother who literally hated him to death."

"You must find a way to smile again. Besides, revenge won't bring Noah back," Liam argued.

His words were greeted with a sly smirk. "Smile. Really? How can I when I feel like I'm dead on the inside? They stole my joy when they killed him. I need that back so I can be the mother Rowan deserves to have. I know there's nothing I can do to bring Noah back, but I sure can see to it the brothers are reunited again," Darby said with conviction.

Before Liam could respond, the waitress came over with utensils and Darby's small glass of cranberry juice. "Your food should be ready soon. Can I get you anything else in the meantime? More coffee?"

"No, I'm good. Thanks," Liam answered.

The waitress walked away, humming a tune.

"There's nothing you can say or do that will stop me," Darby reiterated her stance.

"Noted. Who's next?" Liam asked.

"Big 60," Darby stated.

"Wait. Raymond? The one who was Tyrus's shadow puppet?" Liam was shocked, but not completely surprised.

"Yep. And it won't be easy. I have Intel that Big 60 takes his barking orders from someone who is rarely seen out in public, and when he is, he's always wearing something covering his face. I believe Tyrus had some work done to his face. So he could walk right by us without us knowing." Darby sighed.

"Do you think Raymond will give up Tyrus?" Liam asked, as he made it a point to not call Raymond by what he felt was a stupid street name.

"Nope. He's too loyal. That's why I'm adding a member to the crew," Darby said with reassurance.

"Can this new person be trusted?" Liam was skeptical about adding someone new to the team.

"Yep. Cause he will only know what I need him to know. But his skill set will be invaluable to our mission. Since last night, have you had a chance to speak to Indigo?" Darby wanted to change the discussion, so she attacked Liam's vulnerability.

"No, I'm afraid she won't want to speak to me." Liam gulped down the rest of his coffee.

"I wonder. How does that work over the phone?" Darby pondered.

"Ha. Ha. By text, silly." Liam found humor in her question.

"You need to tell her how you feel about her. She's laid up with probably a broken rib or two, not for Noah, but because she cares about you," Darby said.

"I tried." Liam thought of their kiss. "I kissed her, but she shoved me. Locked herself in the bathroom and come morning had cut her damn hair off."

"You must be an awful kisser," Darby jested.

"Did I see you smile? I'll take it." Liam was pleased to see Darby relax a bit.

"Anyway, Big 60 is our next mark. And none of that macho ground and pound stuff. We take him down by any means." Darby aimed her fingers at Liam.

The waitress brought over their food. She had her shift manager help her with the three entrees Liam had selected from the menu. Darby had only ordered toast and scrambled eggs. She was still feeling uneasy from the panic attack that she'd had. Except for a few delightful grunts of Liam enjoying his food, the two of them ate in silence.

CHAPTER 32: PROFILER

Darby's intent was to get to her therapy session just as it was about to start and not a minute more. She wanted to catch Mike off guard with what she was wearing. The last time she had dressed up to deliberately get the attention of a man was when she and Noah were rekindling the love they once had for one another.

Her jeans hugged her curves perfectly, and the blouse she wore exposed her shoulders. Although her clothes were the initial shiny objects for Mike to see, she knew to seal the deal would take flirtatious gestures and subtle remarks that would have him believe he actually had a chance with her.

Darby took a catwalk around Mike's office. She took time to admire his paintings, university degrees, and some Star Wars toys and action figures that were in the room. "I don't think I ever truly paid attention to what was in your office." Darby walked slowly, but with purpose. She went from one side of the room to the next. Each time she passed his desk, he avoided eye contact. It was his evasiveness and tolerance for her delaying her session that confirmed her suspicions. She had him hooked.

Mike futilely attempted to resist her allure, but Darby had a mystique about her that his profiling instincts couldn't defy. He was trying to make sense of her behavior, but he was having trouble thinking with his PhD brain. He had been having on and off dreams about Darby since he'd first started treating her. She probably would've been cleared to return to duty already if he hadn't had a secret infatuation with her.

Darby didn't take her normal seat in front of his desk. Instead, she moved to the small nailed head brown leather love seat that faced the large window in the room. She hoped that he'd get up and move to the chair that directly faced her. On cue, Mike left his desk chair and sat across from her. Darby finished setting the stage by grabbing a throw pillow that was next to her and positioned it on her lap. She was counting on the pillow serving as a symbolic object that he would fixate his attention on from time to time.

"Right now, he's probably wishing he was the pillow between my legs," Darby thought. "Men are so predictable."

In previous sessions between the two, Mike had taken the reins in what was discussed and showed no swaying emotions in his responses. However, this time he was completely off his game with Darby. He stumbled over his words as he attempted to find an icebreaker to start the meeting. "You look quite … quite different today. Did something change?"

"Besides having a panic attack, I'm feeling quite well," Darby told the half-truth. The panic attack episode had taken her by complete surprise. She had hoped he would bring some clarity to her uncontrolled meltdown. However, she was far from feeling quite well.

"Do you remember what was happening around you just before the anxiety took over your emotions?" Mike questioned.

She didn't hold anything back. "I met up with someone who assisted in the murder of a close friend."

"Were you fearful for your life?" Mike probed deeper.

Darby didn't answer right away. Instead, she began using a breathing technique that Mike had shown her during one of her earlier sessions.

She closed her eyes and thought, "Out with cluttered thoughts …one, two, three … In with pure thinking … four, five, six." Darby focused on her breathing. She wanted to understand what was the cause of her panic attack. After a minute of controlled breathing and internal reasoning, she felt her heart cry. Pure shame overwhelmed her emotions. Then she bawled her eyes out.

Mike didn't do any more than hand Darby the Millennium Falcon tissue box. He knew that she had just discovered an emotion that only she would have to experience and come to terms with it. He discreetly set the timer on his watch to count down seven minutes. If she wasn't able to escape from her feelings, he was prepared to guide her back to a sense of balance.

Darby cried hard tears of regret. Thoughts of that horrific night repeatedly stung her body all over. She twisted and shifted violently in her chair. She felt like she was about to be sick on the rug beneath her. Shame was her shackles. Darby felt like she'd abandoned Noah when he'd needed her the most. Instead of running at the first chance she got, she should've gone back to be by Noah's side. She knew to her core Noah would've stayed with her. Darby felt she should've died that night, too.

More than six minutes elapsed before Darby was able to regain her footing in the present world again. "No, I wasn't scared. Ashamed is more like it." Darby tightly clenched her fists together. "I think I've figured it out."

"Do you mind sharing?" Mike asked.

"Let's just say I won't run away again." Darby was short with her response.

Mike's psychologist intuition prompted him to resist interrupting the space between them with any clever words. Instead, he sat, one leg crossed over the other, and waited for Darby to continue speaking. They sat facing each other for two long and some uncomfortable silent minutes.

"I need your help." Darby didn't want to waste any more time. "I need you to profile someone who I believe had changed his physical appearance."

"Of course. I'm all yours. I mean, I'm in." Mike welcomed the offer.

"Just like that? Don't you want to know more first?" Darby asked.

"Until today, our meetings have been a dog and pony show. You met my questions with responses you felt I needed to hear. But in reality, I wasn't even scratching the surface with you." Mike stood up and peered out the window. "My expertise has been confined to this room. They say I'm helping. They say I'm needed. And the people who I treat should be all the reward needed to keep me going. But they're wrong. Can't they throw me a bone now and then? Well, if you'll have me, I'm your profiler."

Darby smiled in agreement. "I'll be in touch."

Mike was a gentleman and opened his office door for her. He watched her walk by his secretary and out of the building. He closed his office door behind him. Mike walked over to his desk and fished inside one of the drawers. He pulled from it a burner cell phone and texted the only number he was threatened to use. "I'm in."

Tyrus replied, "IT'S ABOUT DAMN TIME!"

"You were right. She knows about you," Mike responded.

"I COULD NOT CARE LESS. DO YOU KNOW THE PLAYERS?"

"Not yet. But I'll have them soon."

"HURRY UP!"

CHAPTER 33: EXAMINATION

Boom! Boom! Boom!

Indigo was awakened from her sleep by a loud banging coming from outside her bedroom. She sat up quickly and was met with severe pain in her abdomen, shoulder, and the cut above her eye. It took a few seconds for the cobwebs to clear in her head before remembering she wasn't back at the hotel. The small, red, oval-shaped clock read 1:07 a.m. By the bright light that was shining through the neutral-colored draperies, Indigo reasoned she had slept past the morning hours.

The noise she heard earlier was consistent and had seemed to get louder. Yet it didn't conceal the soft rhythmic breathing of Kate, who was curled up asleep on the floor. She was wrapped up in a blanket like a burrito. Indigo slowly tapped Kate until her eyes opened.

Kate yawned and stretched out her arms and legs. Her eyes told a story that she hadn't gotten much sleep. "I hope I didn't wake you." Kate stretched again before leaping to her feet. "What time is it?" She heard the banging coming from her front door. "Oh, ginger snap! I'll be right back!"

Kate raced out of the room. She unlocked her front door and yelled down the short hallway, "Ava! I'm here. Sorry."

"You're still the same," Ava jested.

Ava Estrada M.D. was a practicing family physician. She was in her late thirties and pregnant. Ava looked to be in her third trimester. Her petite features were slightly expanded by the many joys of having a baby. She and her partner had tried for several years, but each hopeful attempt had ended with heartbreak and despair. So seeing Ava beaming with a glow of her own was expected.

"I truly appreciate you coming," Kate said.

"That's what friends are for, right?" Ava smiled. "How long has it been since the four of us hit the town?"

"Looking at you, it's been too long," Kate joked. "You look like you could pop any minute."

"My due date is in two weeks. I can't believe we're finally going to be moms." Ava smiled again. "Enough about me. Where's the patient?"

Kate went into the guest room first to explain to Indigo that Ava was there to examine her injuries. Then she ushered Ava into the room and introduced them to each other.

"Hello, Indigo. It's a pleasure to meet you," Ava greeted.

Indigo nodded.

"Oh, yeah. Well, she doesn't talk but can hear everything you say. She communicates with pen and paper," Kate explained.

"Not a problem. Indigo, I want you to lay back and nod whenever you feel pain," Ava requested.

Ava moved her hands over the areas of Indigo's body that showed the most bruising and swelling. She wondered why such an attractive woman had been beaten so harshly.

"It doesn't appear that anything is broken. Have you seen any blood in your urine or stool?" Ava questioned.

Indigo shook her head. Then she motioned she needed to go to the bathroom. When she stood to her feet, the sheet slid down her perfectly fit body and rested on the bed. Indigo walked confidently out of the room in just her T-shirt and underwear. Kate stared off to the opposite corner of the room while Ava's reservations about Indigo grew large wings.

"She's pretty," Ava said, digging for some dirt.

"It's not what you think," Kate defended. "I'm just helping a friend."

"Really? A friend? So, tell me if I'm wrong. Indigo is running from someone so bad that she's scared to go to a hospital. She slept in this room and Tia is unaware of this?" Ava reasoned.

"Sorry, but you're wrong. I don't think she's scared of anyone. And I plan to tell Tia as soon as I get the chance." Kate wanted to change the subject. "Is there anything we should be worried about?"

"It's we now? I thought you were helping a friend." Ava wouldn't let it go. "Unless she comes back and in her silent way tells us that she saw blood in the toilet, you'll need to keep an ice compress on her swelling. And here's a thirty-day supply of Ibuprofen."

Indigo returned to the room. She shook her head to indicate she had not seen any blood.

"That's great news." Ava handed Indigo the bottle of pills. "Take two every six hours and keep some ice on that swelling. You should recover with some rest."

Indigo wrote, *"Thank you."*

Kate walked Ava out to the living room.

"Thank you. I owe you," Kate said sincerely.

"You can pay me back by telling Tia." Ava didn't look back as she exited.

CHAPTER 34: NOT HELPING

It was midday, but Indigo still felt drained. After washing down two pills with bottled water that she had from the night before, she took to the guest bed again. Indigo checked her phone in hopes of receiving a message from Liam, but there was nothing. She was agitated about how they'd sidelined her.

"I microwaved a breakfast sandwich for you." Kate walked in with a plate and a Ziploc bag containing several cubes of ice. "You must be hungry."

Indigo sat up and took the plate from Kate. She closed her eyes for a moment to pray over her food. Then she examined the sandwich.

"It's turkey sausage and egg white," Kate interrupted.

Indigo smiled before taking a bite. Kate sat next to her on the bed. She attempted to place the bag of ice on the side of Indigo's head. Indigo pushed her hand away. The swelling had drastically subsided, but it still had a way to go.

"Sorry. I meant nothing by it." Kate set the bag of ice on the bed and retreated to a chair that was in the room.

Indigo lowered the plate on the bed and wrote, *"Nothing wrong. Just used to caring for myself."*

"I can relate. Do you remember anything from last night?" Kate asked.

Indigo shook her head and went back to eating the breakfast sandwich.

"I came in here because you were crying in your sleep. I thought you were in pain from your injuries, but it looked like you were stuck in a bad dream. Do you want to talk about it?" Kate probed.

"My burden to bear," Indigo scribbled.

"Is it what happened to Mario?" Kate delved deeper. "Sorry, I'm a detective twenty-four/seven."

Indigo couldn't finish the last piece of the sandwich. Her throat felt tight as she fought back a tsunami of tears. She took refuge under the bedsheet.

Kate walked back over to Indigo. She perched herself on the end of the bed near Indigo's head. Then Kate grabbed the bag of melting ice. She placed it on Indigo's head where there was a still a visible lump. "Trust me. I'm not one to give advice, but you shouldn't blame yourself."

"Trust! Do you know what that word means?" Tia startled Kate.

"Tia, this isn't what you think. Let's go into the other room so I can explain," Kate pleaded.

"So you can tell me she's your cousin on your dad's side? All I've done is love your ass. And you do this to me!" Tia was furious. "Ava called me yesterday telling me you needed her to come to your place and today you called in sick. So, as your lover and someone who genuinely cares for you, I come here prepared to nurse you back to health. But what do I get? You playing doctor!"

"Tia, this sucks. I know. But just give me a chance to explain." Kate touched Tia's hand.

"Don't touch me!" Tia shoved Kate hard.

Kate stumbled across the room until finally falling onto her back. Like a turtle flipped on its back, she had a difficult time getting upright again.

Indigo rose from the bed and went right into a fighting stance. She was clearly still less of herself, but she had plenty of fight left in her.

"Indigo, no!" Kate yelled.

"Oh, hell no! Does this B have just her t-shirt and panties on?" Tia ranted.

"Indigo, you're really not helping right now." Kate touched her shoulder. "Please get back in bed and I'm getting you some flannel pajamas to wear." Then she turned her attention towards Tia. "This is upsetting. I get it. But I've earned the right to explain what's going on here. Let's go to the other room."

Tia turned away without saying a word. Kate followed her, but kept a small distance between them.

"Where do I start?" Kate tried gathering her thoughts. "I know you wanted me to let it go—"

"I'll never forgive you," Tia interrupted. Then she threw Kate's spare key hard at the wall leading towards the front door. It got lodged in a canvas painting of a multicolored vase full of sunflowers. She left without giving Kate the satisfaction of seeing her cry.

Kate yelled for Tia to come back, but she was out of sight in a matter of seconds. Although she had tried in the past to break off their relationship, Kate never imagined hurting Tia in such a cruel way. She slammed the door and snatched her cellphone from the charging unit. Kate texted Darby in all caps, "SUPER ATHLETIC MODEL JUST COST ME MY RELATIONSHIP … I BETTER BE ON THE TEAM." It didn't take too long before she saw that her message had been read and it appeared that Darby was typing a response.

Indigo walked out of the room, still in her t-shirt and underwear. She wanted to check on Kate. Once she saw that Kate was alone and in no imminent danger, Indigo gestured that she was sorry.

"You're still not helping," Kate uttered as she avoided eye contact with the sexy bombshell.

"LOL, welcome to the team," Darby texted.

CHAPTER 35: MEETING PLACE

Several days had passed since Big 60 had Rip and Cord check-in. He still felt somewhat responsible for the dangerous initiation that Tyrus had them face to prove their loyalty. Big 60 needed to prepare them for a future hit that Tyrus was planning. He didn't know what, but something ominous was lurking in the shadows.

Strangely, Tyrus had kept him in the dark about what was happening next, yet the signs were in plain view. Tyrus wasn't the best at concealing his feelings, especially when he felt threatened. Big 60 noticed that he had started wearing a mask all the time, even when it was just the two of them. Tyrus also had Big 60 beef up security detail in several of the New York and New Jersey locations and was only available to others by phone.

Big 60's role of being the top dog had taken on new meaning. With the absence of the mask man present at the prearranged face-to-face meetings, the street connects and gun suppliers thought there were two unmarked gravesites somewhere out there—one for that ridiculous mask and the other for the idiot who wore it. Ironically, no one was spooked by the masked man's disappearance, so business ran accordingly.

Although operations seemed to be going on without any unusual glitches, Tyrus's erratic behavior made him extremely unpredictable and dangerous. It was like reaching your hand inside a burlap bag containing a trapped rattlesnake, and the anticipation of getting bitten was far worse than the toxic venom. Big 60 couldn't free his mind from the uneasiness of not knowing Tyrus's next move. His requested meeting with Rip and Cord was something he felt would give him an escape from his troubled thoughts.

Cord and Mel were the first two waiting at the meeting point. Cord sat on a park bench and the way his head moved from one side to the next indicated Mel was pacing back and forth. They were in a full-blown conversation. Other park goers stared oddly at a man sitting alone on a bench talking loudly at times and laughing abruptly.

Mel spotted Big 60 coming up from behind. Cord greeted him with a simple nod of his head.

"Have you seen Rip?" Big 60 asked.

"Not yet. But she knows about the meeting," Cord replied.

Big 60 smiled at Cord's attire. When they first had met, he was wearing clothes that a man twice his age would wear, but now he had on a pair of ripped jeans and a thin sweater with Scooby Doo etched in it. "Pardon my rudeness. Mel, it's good to see you, too."

"What up, bro?" Mel always took pleasure in being recognized whenever someone other than Cord acknowledged his existence.

"Can I help you with anything?" Rip seemed to appear from nowhere and offered to help Big 60 with what he was carrying in his hands and over his shoulders.

"Yeah. Thanks," Big 60 answered.

He unloaded the three individually bagged camping chairs off his broad shoulders. Rip tossed two over to Cord, one for him and the other for Mel to carry.

"Over there," Big 60 pointed.

Big 60 followed behind his two disciples. He was beaming with pride, but knew Rip was different ever since what happened in Baltimore. He didn't let on that her new choice of hair coloring was definitely a bold statement. She went from dark black to fire engine red. He knew Tyrus would have something to say about it, but at that point, he didn't care. Big 60 even ignored the fact that Rip came concealing her gun and knives. He had told them before they met to leave their gardening tools home. "Did she lose trust in me too?" he whispered under his breath.

Rip turned around to face Big 60. "What're we going to do? Sit in a circle and hold hands in the park?"

"Ha. Ha." Big 60 laughed. "Better than that. We're gonna have a barbecue."

Big 60 had brought everything needed to grill in the park. They feasted on steak and chicken kabobs and quenched their palates with medium-grade bottles of wine. Surprisingly, it was Cord who was the grill master of the three. They sat in the park for hours. Their random conversations ping ponged back and forth without any serious intentions. Big 60 had been momentarily freed from the nagging worries that had taken unwanted residency in his head.

It was getting late, and they'd each had their fair share of wine. Big 60 was buzzed, but still had his wits about him.

"What we do isn't easy. Faces and places will become dark images you won't care to recognize. You're constantly on alert and trust becomes a five-letter word used only by fools who dig their own graves. But if you're lucky, you won't go completely numb. As best as you can, cherish those rare faces and places that keep you feeling alive." Big 60 sighed heavily. "No matter what, intentionally or not, don't betray the images you see. Cause if you do, Lady Karma will haunt you for the rest of your life or grant you mercy and end you quickly."

Cord and Mel were lightweights when it came to consuming alcohol. They were listening, but incapable of understanding what the hell Big 60 was trying to convey to them. On the other hand, Rip never lost her edge. Until hearing his rant, she wondered why, since the night in Baltimore, he had treated them like two elves on the shelf to be played with at his leisure. Rip wanted in on the action. She'd proved her loyalty to him, but instead he had been distant.

"Is this our goodbye meal?" Rip inquired.

Her words were sobering to Cord and Mel. They were now fully attentive.

"No. Not at all," Big 60 answered.

"Good. You did say if I wanted my life to change, to go with you. Well, I want it to change." Rip wanted Big 60 to know she wasn't shaken up about the ambush his masked boss had arranged.

"There's something big coming. I don't know what. But be ready," Big 60 stated.

CHAPTER 36: QUESTIONS

Darby and Mike met on two separate occasions so he could drill her for answers about Tyrus. His questions ranged from which hand he wrote with to the things that interested him. The meetings were held at a local Brooklyn diner. The meetings lasted as long as their meal went. Mike tried to eat slower each time, but Darby still would ask for the check about thirty minutes after they received their meals.

Liam was on Big 60 watch. He managed to follow him to a park where he sat and ate with two people—neither being Tyrus. He always seemed to lose Big 60 in traffic, but was gathering intel on his specific habits.

Each day that Mike had nothing new to tell Tyrus was a day closer to his demise. He knew so because Tyrus told Mike he'd make him suffer first, then make him unrecognizable to his pathetic family. Mike had to do something quickly or try to go into hiding. Having a target on his back for the rest of his life wasn't an option he wanted to choose.

"I have what you've given me, but I'm going to need more information about Tyrus. Do you have any more pictures of him than the ones you provided? Is there anyone else who can answer some questions for me?" Mike inquired, with his life on the line.

Darby didn't think it was an unusual request, but was hesitant to let Mike meet other team members and, more importantly, wanted to avoid Aunty Cynthia at all costs. "Tomorrow I'll text you an address with a time to meet," Darby responded.

The next day, Darby arranged for Mike to meet her at Aunty Cynthia's place. When he pulled up to the house, he noticed Darby wasn't alone. Liam was standing alongside her in the carport area of the house. Darby had already grabbed the spare key that Noah once told her Aunty Cynthia hid inside a fake rock. They had the run of the house for about two hours. Darby had asked her parents to invite Aunty Cynthia to a lunch date with Rowan. It was an easy sell, because

Rowan and Aunty Cynthia were becoming inseparable. Her father was instructed to text before they left the kid-friendly restaurant.

"Liam, this is Mike, our profiler." Darby kept the introduction formal and short.

"Aren't you the UFC heavyweight champion?" Mike beamed at the man he had come to admire. He vigorously shook Liam's hand. "I've been following your career." Mike pretended to dodge a punch. "Don't hurt me, champ. Ha. Ha."

"He's a spirited one, ain't he?" Liam said with a wry smirk.

"I'll make sure you get his autograph. Now we don't have much time," Darby whispered. "Anything you touch, you must put back in its original place."

Darby appeared all business, but actually she was anxious about going into the house filled with photos and other memories of Noah. Aunty Cynthia's home had a familiar smell. On the coffee table, there was an eight by ten framed photo of the night Noah was drafted number one in the NFL. Next to it was a recent picture of Rowan tightly hugging Aunty Cynthia. She picked up the pink-framed photo and lost herself in her daughter's smile. She compared both pictures, realizing her daughter shared the same smile as her father.

"Where do you want me to start?" Mike interrupted.

He had put aside his man crush for Liam to begin reasoning who was Tyrus. Mike had a vested interest, and his life depended upon helping Darby and her crew get to Tyrus before his usefulness was no longer needed.

Darby pointed towards the room in which she had last a FaceTime session with Noah. She remained focused on the photo that she carefully held in her hands. Mike scurried into the room without haste.

"She's a good-looking kid." Liam complimented the picture of Rowan. "Someone was looking out for her cause she has two ugly parents."

"Ha. Ha." Darby actually laughed.

"I know being here isn't easy for you. But we're going to need your help. You need to tell him what to look for," Liam voiced with sincerity.

For about forty-five minutes, Darby pointed and Mike did a mental scan and took notes. He was intent on coming up with a profile that would help him identify the person who seemed to hold his life in the balance.

They left Aunty Cynthia's home before Darby's parents left the restaurant. Mike was content with the information he had and was feeling good that he would be able to accurately profile the man who was threatening him over the phone. Aunty Cynthia's home was meticulously left undisturbed.

Though Mike had significant information to draw conclusions of the possible identity of the threatening masked man, he looked forward to ending the night interviewing Liam about what extra details he could add.

Darby took Liam to the same Brooklyn diner she and Mike had been meeting in.

"I see we have an extra guest tonight. Will your usual table work?" The waitress who served them on the two other occasions was also taking on the role of hostess.

Darby nodded, and then the three of them followed behind the particularly chipper waitress to their table.

"I'll be right back with another menu and some coffee." Their waitress took off towards the coffee station.

Liam and Darby sat on the same side, facing the entrance. Mike took the seat right across from Liam, so the two of them were facing each other. They appeared to be like two opposite bookends; one muscular and having a definite spine, while the other was a few sheets of paper that had been folded together.

Mike was familiar with the limited time he would have, so once the waitress came back and took their orders, he peppered Liam with questions. He had hoped to gather what he needed before the food arrived, so he could simply talk to one of his favorite UFC fighters.

Darby had already given Liam the perimeters to work within as he disclosed what he knew about Tyrus. Basically, he wasn't to share anything about why or how he got involved and to say very little about Noah. Darby listened to Liam saying "next" whenever one of Mike's probing questions crossed the line.

"Lucky for you guys, we aren't as busy tonight." Their waitress had another server help with bringing out their orders. "Here's your food. At this time, is there anything else I can get you?"

Liam politely waved off the waitress. Some of his plates of food were set on the empty portion of the table next to Mike, so Darby would have space for her small plate of chicken salad. Liam shoveled food into his mouth.

"Hi, teammates." Kate took the seat next to Mike.

Darby pretended she wasn't caught off guard by Kate's presence.

"There's someone back home angry with you." Kate directed her attention to Liam, then back to Darby. "Is this our profiler?"

"I see we have another guest." The waitress came quickly over to their table with a menu for Kate. "It must be double date night."

"He should be so lucky," Kate commented.

"I'm right here. I can hear you," Mike jested at being offended.

"Nothing for her. We were just leaving," Darby said to the waitress.

Liam spoke with bits of food flying out of his mouth. "Really? I still have two plates to get through."

"No, you stay here. I'll get a ride with our teammate. Besides, he's man-crushing on you anyway." Darby motioned for Kate to leave with her.

"Again! I can hear you," Mike repeated.

CHAPTER 37: CONFESSIONS

Darby sat quietly in Kate's jeep, still wondering not only how Kate tracked them to that Brooklyn diner, but also why she wanted to limit Mike's access to the team. There was something about Mike that made her guarded.

"I didn't like who I was the day we met," Darby confessed.

"No worries. I didn't help matters. I was a bit smug." Kate made fun of herself. "Look at me. I can shoot a gun."

"Ha. Ha." They laughed away the tension that had formed an unhealthy barrier between them.

"I know what I'm doing is wrong, but it's the only thing that is keeping me from losing my shit. No therapist, not my parents, not even my daughter can help me erase my mistake with Noah. He's dead because of me." Darby unloaded a ton of remorseful feelings onto Kate.

"My therapist, before I slammed his head into a wall for trying to get touchy with me, would say we are suffering from survivor's remorse. That's the guilt and blame that you're feeling," Kate said, trying to console her teammate.

"Maybe for you. But I know if Noah knew he had a daughter, he would've done everything to protect her. Not risk losing her to fulfill a reckless promise he made to his father," Darby countered.

"Kind of what we're doing now," Kate mumbled.

"We both swore to uphold the law and here we are being judge and jury," Darby retorted.

There was a brief moment when all that was heard were the windshield wipers going as it had begun to rain. Then, in unison, they turned and faced each other and both said, "I'm the judge!"

Again, laughter filled the car.

"How's it going with your Black girl?" Darby jested.

"That's way not cool." Kate raised her hand up to dismiss Darby's insensitive joke. "My partner and I have definitely seen better days. And here I thought you and I were getting past our rough patch."

"We have, but I couldn't resist," Darby smirked. "Seriously, have you apologized yet?"

"I've tried, but at work it's been uncomfortable as she won't look my way or stand still long enough to hear me out. And she doesn't accept my calls or reply to my texts." Kate believed she'd exhausted all options.

"Her avoidance could mean either two things. One, she's still crazy in love with you so you still have a chance, or, two, she's truly done with you," Darby speculated.

"Tell me something I don't know," Kate said sarcastically.

"Do you own a pair of boxing gloves?" Darby asked.

"What?" Kate was confused about what Darby was asking.

"Listen, if you have a pair, great. If not, go out and buy a pair and the next time you see her, toss them at her. Then tell her to put the gloves on and she can hit you as much as she wants, as long as she stays to hear you out," Darby explained.

"Nah, I'll pass. Signing up to be a punching bag just isn't my thing." Kate wasn't going to entertain Darby's suggestion.

"Gloves or no gloves, just promise me you'll try again and again. She deserves to hear the truth. Once she's heard it, then it's up to her what she does with it," Darby pleaded.

"I guess," Kate said shyly.

"No, promise me!" Darby didn't want Kate to make the same mistake she had made with Noah.

"Since you're in your feelings right now, I'll go with it. I'll keep trying." Kate didn't want to ruin their recent breakthrough. "So where to?"

"A party." While at a stop sign, Darby entered an address into the jeep's GPS.

The GPS calculated it would take twenty minutes to arrive at their destination. Darby was taking Kate to Mercedes Williams, the uncouth woman's apartment who was charged with Tyrus's sham of a *Banging Party* home going. After doing some surveillance on her, Darby had determined Mercedes was a dead end. Tyrus and Big 60 were never seen to come or go from her residence. Since the payout she received for being Tyrus's sole facilitator of his affairs, she'd been running from one male cash opportunity to the next.

"Promise me you'll come back to this apartment and shake it upside down until you know how much change is lost in her couch." Darby was preparing for the absolute worst.

"I'm sitting here now because I promised Detective Nine, my mentor, that I'd get those responsible for the Brooklyn Blitz. She gave her life for me," Kate reflected. "Let's plan to check that couch together."

CHAPTER 38: THE CALL

Ring. Ring.

Mike held his burner phone to his ear. He waited patiently to hear a specific voice on the other end. He finally had some information that should give him a fighting chance to escape with his life.

"Don't waste my time!" Tyrus seemed agitated about the call.

"Hello. It's me." Mike was antsy.

"Me, get on with it." Tyrus's lack of patience for Mike was about a popcorn seed away from popping.

"I know her players." Mike's mouth ran a personal best one-hundred-yard dash. "She's partnered with Liam O'Carroll, a UFC fighter. Not just a fighter, but he's the heavyweight champion. Then there's his corner girl, who goes by the name of Indigo. And the female detective who was the lone survivor of the Brooklyn Blitz—Kate Lawson." Mike searched his thoughts for any more information he had that would possibly provide him a life preserver with Tyrus. "That's all I got."

Tyrus almost wet his pants with excitement. He had feared Darby was working with the Bureau, but to hear she was tracking him off the books was poetic justice. He was just given the green light to finally exterminate the one person who not only wouldn't give up searching for him, but worse, Darby was a constant reminder of his brother. Once Darby and her team were gone forever, he planned to do the same to Aunty Cynthia.

Click.

CHAPTER 39: STATEMENT

"Pick up! Pick up!" Tyrus didn't waste any time setting his plan in motion. Whisper would be his eyes in the sky and cover his back. But he needed him to scare off the NYPD detective. The streets were already an agitated beehive with the men and women in Blue. Tyrus didn't want to draw any unnecessary attention to his underworld of gun and drug smuggling.

"Lima Charlie?" Whisper asked.

"Yep. The line is clear." Tyrus tried to conceal his excitement, but the thought of finally ridding himself of Darby was too much to bear. "It's time to cut out our final weed, but first I need you to get that last detective from the Brooklyn Blitz to back off. I don't want any more heat on us."

"You don't think murdering an FBI agent won't bring problems?" Whisper questioned.

"My mole says she working off the books. They'll think her PTSD got the better of her. Now, you go and make a statement to get that detective to stay in her place." Tyrus kept the call short.

Whisper spared Tyrus the news that he had already been in contact with his little mouse and it was going to be darn near impossible to get her to back down, but he had a plan. It was sure to get her attention.

CHAPTER 40: BOXING GLOVES

Tia had changed her shift to avoid seeing her ex-lover. The thought of Kate's betrayal was still too fresh of a wound to begin the process of healing. Though she had more seniority at her rank than the other lieutenant on the force, she took the night shift. She was sitting at her desk reviewing notes left from the day shift when Kate stormed into her office.

"Tia, we need to talk." Kate locked the office door behind her.

"It's lieutenant! You don't get a pass today, Detective Lawson." Tia's emotions went from zero to 120 in seconds. "You will not ambush me at work."

"Hello. You must've forgotten. I'm Kate and you're Tia. We love each other. Ring a bell?" Kate was being ornery.

"Girl, please!" Tia said through clenched teeth. "Get out of my office before you get the street version of me."

Tia tried to keep her professional composure, but Kate knew the right buttons not just to push, but also to crush. Actually, it was Tia who she wanted to talk to, not the rational Lt. Marks.

Thump.

"Put these on!" Kate took a pair of red boxing gloves out of the bag she was holding and tossed them at Tia.

"Girl, you going to bring a fight to a fighter? You should've started with this." Tia stood up and kicked off her high heels and, like a pro, stuffed her hands into the gloves with ease. She used her teeth to secure the second glove to her dominant right hand.

"You can hit me as long as you give me a chance to say my piece," Kate pleaded.

Tia quickly closed the distance and snapped Kate's head back with a solid left-handed jab to her face.

"Ouch!" Kate was stunned; not that Tia punched her, but she'd actually hit her in the face. "You're really mad. I knew boxing gloves weren't a good idea. Please, do not hit the face."

"Mad? I'm pissed." Tia threw a barrage of wild punches—repeatedly hitting Kate's shoulders. "I gave you my heart! You didn't take care of it!"

Kate had exhaustedly rehearsed what she would say, but from the numbing pain in both arms and the desperate look on her lover's face, she did the one thing that came naturally. She leaned into an unguarded Tia and kissed her on the lips, forehead, and cheeks. Kate repeated the rotation of tiny kisses and light touches as long as Tia would allow. The sting from her bruised lip hurt, but the kisses against Tia's ebony skin and soft lips were soothing.

"No. No. No." Tia wanted to pull away, but her lover's sweet touches had such a magnetic pull on her. Her arms went limp. She was like a boxer in the last round of an intense bout, too spent to keep fighting.

In between the gentle kisses, Kate whispered, "The woman you saw at my place—we're on a team together to take down the rest of the people responsible for the Brooklyn Blitz."

Tia came to life. "Are you crazy. That's too … dangerous."

Kate smothered Tia's words with a barrage of fluttering kisses. "I love you so much."

"Oh, yeah. We love you too!" The night shift officers who were still in the building hooped and hollered as they watched Lt. Marks and Detective Lawson embrace in a sensual lip lock.

"Okay, break it up. The show is over." Shyly, Lt. Marks took control of the situation.

"Lieutenant, let's get out of here. I'll tell you more over a few drinks." Kate was excited to have Tia back in her life.

"I'll follow you. Wait! Did you buy sleeping beauty pajamas?" Tia asked.

"Two layered wool pajamas," Kate jested.

The two of them left the station with a few catcalls sounding loudly behind them. Tia and Kate took separate cars. They agreed to meet at their favorite quaint bar. It was the same one where the two of them had once sung karaoke throughout the night. It was the same song each time, *Like I'm Gonna Lose You* by Meghan Trainor and John Legend. Tia took on the vocals of Meghan and Kate did her best impersonation of John. The unusually packed bar goers gave them standing ovations after each rendition. Their love for each other was obvious.

Kate waited for Tia to bring her car around. She felt giddy, like a teenage girl going on her first date. She searched for their karaoke favorite and streamed it from her cellphone to play through her jeep radio. Soon she saw Tia's headlights flash in her rearview mirror.

Ring! Ring!

An unknown number flashed across her jeep's touch screen. At first she thought about allowing the call to go to voicemail, but she thought it could've been Darby calling from a burner phone. Kate answered the call, but waited for the person on the other end to speak first.

"Little mousy, are you listening?" Whisper seemed excited.

Kate immediately recognized his voice.

"I need you to stay focused on one thing or the other." Whisper got right to the point.

Thump! Beeeeeeeeeep!

Kate didn't get a chance to process what Whisper meant because Tia had crashed into the rear of her jeep and her horn was blaring nonstop. Kate operated on pure instinct. She leaped from her vehicle and ran to Tia's car. Tia was slumped over the steering wheel. Her petite body was heavy enough to cause the horn to continuously sound off. Kate pulled her lover from the car. She slid to the ground with Tia who had been shot, and was struggling to breathe in her arms.

"Help me! Help me!" Kate screamed. "No, baby. Hold on. Help!"

CHAPTER 41: MY LOVE

The next morning, Darby called in a small favor to get Mike's home address. She didn't care if her inquiry would draw any suspicions from her superiors. Her innate investigative senses said he was the mole and the reason Tia was in critical care, fighting for her life.

Just before noon, Liam kicked opened Mike's front door of a modest-looking apartment. Darby was the first to enter with her throwaway gun drawn. Indigo followed right behind her and was armed, too. Liam covered their six with a shotgun that seemed fitting for his massive stature. Kate was not part of the raid. She hadn't left Tia's side since the attempted murder.

Darby's tactical training was on full display. She and Indigo cleared rooms quickly before the two found Mike's lifeless body still tied securely to a chair in his bedroom. It had appeared that he was tortured until being asphyxiated from a plastic bag that was still fastened over his head.

"Damn!" Darby was frustrated with herself. "Tyrus knows I have a daughter."

"Don't worry. We'll get him," Liam reassured Darby.

Indigo patted Darby on her shoulder to endorse what Liam had just said.

"This sorry piece of shit told Tyrus about the team. Damn!" Darby beat herself up with guilt.

Snap. Snap.

Indigo snapped her fingers in front of Darby's face and then pointed around the room. Darby understood there was no time for her self-pity. They needed to search Mike's apartment for any clues about Tyrus's identity.

Though the ceiling light was busted in his bedroom, there was still a fair amount of light coming from behind the curtains. However, Indigo wanted more light, so she walked over to fully open the blinds.

"No!" Darby asserted. "Sniper. Could be an ambush."

Indigo backed away from the window. Then the three of them went around Mike's living space looking for anything that would help with figuring out anything about Tyrus. They used the light on their cellphones for additional lighting. Fifteen minutes had gone by without anything being of a significant find. Mike's laptop and cellphone were missing, or more like taken.

Buzz. Buzz.

They were just about to call off the search when Darby's phone vibrated in her pocket. Her screen flashed—unknown caller. She accepted the call.

"You and Noah thought you were smart. But I'm the dealer who holds all the cards," Tyrus gloated.

"I'm going to kill you!" Darby squeezed the phone as she spoke.

"Tisk. Tisk. Hasn't anyone taught you phone etiquette?" Tyrus was still feeling like he had the upper hand. "Noah had you listed in his phone as *My Love*. Pitiful!"

"You don't get to say his name!" Darby yelled.

"Let me guess. Cause if I do, you gonna kill me, right? Blah. Blah. Blah. Let me get to the point cause you boring me. You want me? In two days at sunset, meet me where it all started," Tyrus said, smirking behind his mask.

"You so damn original. I see you're still fantasizing about those crime and mob movies. Sunset? For once, grow up!" Darby goaded.

Tyrus hated being mocked or being the subject of someone's joke. He started to lose his cool. "Show or don't show." Tyrus ended the call.

Bang! Bang! Bang!

Darby discharged three shots into Mike's lifeless body. The impact shifted the weight of his body, causing him to fall onto his side. Indigo waved her arms in the air as if to motion, "What's going on?"

"They all must die!" Darby said as she exited Mike's bedroom.

CHAPTER 42: BLOOD BROTHER

Tyrus called a meeting with Big 60. The two met at the same apartment Big 60 had lived in as a child. It was one of a few apartments rented by one of Tyrus's dummy corporations. The place was furnished but smelled like it hadn't been lived in for months. Big 60 walked around the place where he had once ate, slept, and struggled against the monsters in his head.

"Why here?" Big 60 wondered.

"Do you remember what happened here?" Tyrus took a seat on the couch.

"More than you know. There are fond memories, and some I wish not to recall." Big 60 was a bit uncomfortable as he left his old bedroom.

"It's right here we became blood brothers." Tyrus removed his mask. "You've been a brother to me more than anyone."

Big 60 had seen Tyrus without his mask several times, but it still shocked him that the familiar voice was coming from a stranger's face. The two didn't seem to go together.

"We are still brothers from another mother. Did something change?" Big 60 questioned.

"Nah. Just like twins at birth, I'm making sure we still joined at the hip. I feel like Noah's death divided us." Tyrus waited to see Big 60's reaction.

Big 60's body language and facial expression didn't reveal any of his true thoughts. Though he felt Noah's death was bad karma, Big 60 waved off Tyrus's statement, as if it was completely unfounded.

"Good to know. It's time to take out Darby and her crew," Tyrus said with conviction.

"You found her?" Big 60 was stunned.

Tyrus told him that he'd had eyes on her for about a month. Big 60 questioned why he had kept that secret from him. Tyrus didn't mince words, as he was brutally honest about how Big 60 had seemed caught in his feelings with the death of Noah and Tyrus's desire to end Aunty Cynthia's useless life.

"Noah was one thing, but Aunty Cynthia? What did she do?" Big 60 questioned.

"She loved him and didn't hide her distaste for me. Do you know what it's like living in the shadow of your little brother? I felt suffocated. Like two hands were constantly squeezing my neck tighter and tighter. She could've helped. I needed someone to offer me oxygen. Instead, she put her foot on my throat with sly remarks and endless praises for her favorite nephew." Tyrus balled up his fists. "I need air to breathe. As long as she's alive, her foot remains on my throat."

"You know, back then, we both didn't make it easy for anyone to love us." Big 60 tried to lighten the mood.

"Funny. Besides, she has what's rightfully mine." Tyrus didn't lose his focus.

"Uh. You're legally dead. Remember?" Big 60 reminded him of the obvious. "The money and laundromats wouldn't go to you."

"Money I have, and living my dad's sorry ass dream is the last thing I want to do. Nah. I want the ultimate payback." Tyrus paused a moment to add to the suspense before revealing his final secret. "I have a niece."

Big 60 was speechless. He knew Tyrus only had one brother, so Noah had a child that he didn't know existed. To him, karma just tightened the snare that constricted his breathing.

"Are you going to hurt the child?" Big 60 questioned the unthinkable.

Tyrus laughed. "I'm not a monster. Once Darby is gone, her parents and Aunty Cynthia will be next. I'm gonna raise my niece as if she was mine. Besides, I couldn't hurt anyone named after my mother."

"Not a monster at all," Big 60 said sarcastically. "Did Noah know he had a daughter?"

"Nope. Darby kept her a secret. But nothing stays hidden from me," Tyrus boasted. "Now, I'm going to need all hands on deck, especially my true brother. Are you in?"

Big 60 wrestled in his head with the news of Darby and Noah having a child and Tyrus's plan to wipe out the little girl's immediate kin just to raise her as his own. He had mixed feelings, but he stayed loyal to Tyrus.

"I've never been out. I'm here to the end," Big 60 confirmed his allegiance. "Where do we find her?"

"In two days, they come to us. I got her number from the phone we took off Noah. I destroyed it so no one tracks us." Tyrus handed him a note. "Here's the address where everything goes down. Make sure those two minions of yours are there, too. I'll make sure Whisper has an eye in the sky."

"You got it! All hands on deck," Big 60 confirmed.

CHAPTER 43: SURVEILLANCE

Later that night, Big 60 drove aimlessly around Brooklyn before stopping at the site where the battle would take place in two days. It was formerly a public school that couldn't sustain student enrollment due to magnet and charter schools that attracted the local residences and stole state funds too. The building had seen better days and had remained vacant for over ten years. Selling it was a low priority with the city officials.

The structure looked sound, but there were too many broken windows to count. It took up a large amount of real estate. At its peak, the building housed students from sixth to ninth grade, with an average of twenty-five students per classroom. Though it was tucked away in the community, it still had multiple entries and exits—two things Big 60 didn't favor.

He parked his luxury SUV at a distance he could survey the abandoned school, as well as the surrounding community. He left it running but turned off the headlights. Except for an occasional car driving by and teenagers taking a shortcut to get somewhere else, the area was relatively quiet. There were no signs that Darby and her crew were watching him.

Big 60 found some humor in the faint thought of possibly dying in a school in the States instead of during one of his three tours in Iraq. His veteran disability benefits had gone from sixty percent to one hundred percent. He suffered greatly from Post-Traumatic Stress Disorder (PTSD) and injuries during reconnaissance and abstraction missions. He was a trained killer who, like some military members, learned to enjoy bringing the chaos and pain to others.

He grabbed his cellphone and texted Rip and Cord the money-mouth face emoji. It meant he had a job for them. As if they were sitting by their phones waiting to hear from him, two hug emojis were simultaneously fired back at him, meaning they accepted. He ended the conversation by sending them the face with the head bandage, meaning to arm up and show no mercy.

CHAPTER 44: ROOFTOP

Darby, Indigo, and Liam drove up to the school a little after eight in the evening. They all wore bulletproof vests and had about ten pounds of extra ammo stored in pockets and on belts clips. Except for Liam, the other two wore blue baseball hats. Liam was in the driving seat while Darby sat shotgun. Indigo observed the surroundings from the backseat.

The sky was reddish brown. It was an ominous sight to the expected bloodshed that was presumed to happen. Darby had acquired an armored SUV to drive up to the school that she'd once walked the halls with her ninth-grade sweetheart, Noah Boss.

Tyrus waited at the entrance of the school. He was wearing a Jason Voorhees white hockey mask with streaks of red paint that resembled blood. He opened his arms wide and yelled over, "Time to get schooled!"

Darby finally had eyes on the man she wanted to bury more than anything. There was no feeling of a panic attack coming on. Pure anger electrified her body and senses. She shifted in her seat with her gun at the ready. "This fool is always grandstanding," she thought.

Liam spied her reactions. "Stick to the plan. Don't get out."

Tyrus had a captive audience and was up to the task of performing for them. He kneeled down on both knees and pretended to pray. He looked up at the sky and yelled, "Happy birthday, Noah."

Bang! Bang!

If he'd wanted to say more, he couldn't, because Darby bounded from the car, shooting in his direction. Tyrus fled into the building. Their front windshield took two direct hits. Whisper tried to take out the driver, but the bulletproof glass held strong. Liam drove the car alongside Darby to shield her from sniper fire that seemed to come from the left. Indigo exited from the rear, on the passenger's side, to aid Darby in the fight. The two disappeared into the building. Gunfire ensued from inside the school.

Liam raced frantically from the car without any concern for his own life. He couldn't allow anything to happen to Indigo. He knew she was risking her life to support him. He was only a few feet from the entrance, but still far enough away for Whisper to possibly drop him before he made it to the front door.

"I determine who lives or dies. Today, you … Ewwww! That shit burns," Whisper said, as he still managed to squeeze out two less than accurate shots. The bullet from Detective Lawson's gun had punched a quarter-sized hole in his back and taken up residence in his abdomen.

"Go!" Detective Lawson called into her radio.

Unmarked cars and tactical vehicles sped in from all directions. Headlights lit up the area like the sun came back out to see what was happening. Detective Lawson had no trouble convincing her chief to execute an order to take down the men responsible for the attempted murder of Lt. Marks. He called in favors from other precincts to make a definite statement: if you mess with one, you mess with us all.

"Little mousy, you couldn't stay away," Whisper grimaced as he spoke. His shirt was stained with a steady flow of blood. "Didn't think you were one to shoot someone in the back."

"That's funny, coming from a guy who makes a living hiding in the shadows, waiting to pick off people from a distance. You were so predictable about going for the driver," Detective Lawson proclaimed her deductions.

Whisper continued to rest in his prone position. His hands were still attached to his rifle. "That's right. You were in the car when I shot the chubby detective. He screamed like someone took his last piece of apple pie. Ha. Ha."

Bang!

Detective Lawson put a bullet into Whisper's leg.

"Damn you!" Whisper released his grip on the rifle. He took in two deep breaths before speaking again. "Is that the best you got? Cause if it is, I'm going to make you eat that gun."

"Face me, you coward! Tia had nothing to do with this!" Detective Lawson was growing tired of hearing him speak.

Whisper struggled to turn over, but eventually was able to make it onto his back. He wrestled with freeing his watch from his wrist. Whisper placed it on the ground next to him. He spat some blood on the ground. Then he looked directly at Detective Lawson. "I knew you'd be the one."

Detective Lawson finally had the man who was responsible for the deaths of her comrades and the attempted murder of her lover. But still hesitated about executing the final blow.

"The day I took out that dirty detective, I knew. You were the only one during the chaos to look up for me. You were determined to find me." He began to wheeze as he spoke. "You didn't even take cover. I admired that, so I obliged you by making myself seen. Finish what you came here to do." Whisper took his attention off Detective Lawson.

The tension increased between the two. Whisper didn't hide the fact that he would reach for something. Detective Lawson tightened her stance and grip on her gun.

"Only one of us will leave this rooftop alive." Whisper motioned towards his pants leg.

Bang! Bang!

Detective Lawson put two fatal bullets into his chest. He fell flat on his back with one hand still pointing like he had a gun.

CHAPTER 45: HOMEROOM

Indigo managed to catch up to Darby. They moved swiftly and carefully through the hallways of the school. Like the game of Whack-a-Mole, gunmen sprouted out from dark corners, empty classrooms, and janitor closets. Darby and Indigo reacted quickly to shooting and killing many of their assailants. They were also aided by the tactical team's marksmen, who were clearing rooms from the outside windows and helped them avoid getting shot.

Liam ran into the building. He saw lifeless bodies sprawled out all along the hallways. He was thankful that none were Indigo or Darby. But he still felt uneasy. The school was larger than he thought. He didn't know which direction they had gone or where to go, so he decided to just follow the bodies.

Darby moved with purpose. She had a strong suspicion Tyrus couldn't resist doing something dramatic, so she followed her instincts. She had remembered he told her they would meet where it all started. It wasn't just the school, but the homeroom where she and Noah met for the first time. Her love for Noah was the compass that guided her back to their ninth-grade homeroom.

More and more members of the NYPD were gaining control of the school. Tyrus's men were either freely giving up or losing their lives in battle. The NYPD suffered some casualties, but it wasn't enough to deter them from their mission.

"Where the hell are Rip and Cord?" Tyrus said worriedly.

"They should be arriving soon," Big 60 reassured him.

"They better be. It was supposed to be all hands on deck." Tyrus threw his arms in the air.

Big 60 motioned for Tyrus to be silent. He heard someone coming.

Darby crept up slowly. The door was closed, and there wasn't enough light to see into the room. She retrieved a small flashlight from her vest pocket. She held her gun in one hand and in the other, the flashlight. She signaled for Indigo to open the door with her free hand.

Darby counted down from three. She rushed into the room with the flashlight emanating light in the dark room. Her eyes quickly examined the corner of the room where she and Noah once sat as googly-eyed teenagers.

Big 60 came from the rear. He kicked Indigo in the back as she fiddled with getting her flashlight from her own vest. Indigo went crashing into Darby, causing her to drop her gun. Indigo took two bullets to her center mass, before she could get off a single shot. She tumbled over a few desks and chairs.

Darby tried reaching for her gun, but Big 60 yanked her back by her shoulders. The two of them went into hand-to-hand combat. At different points in the fight, each had gotten the better of the other. Except for a busted nose and lip, Big 60's blows were more punishing, but Darby wouldn't concede.

"I didn't know he was going to kill Noah," Big 60 confessed. "I was just about to get Noah to get Chameleon out in the open."

"This ain't the movies and I'm not your priest. So save your confessions for someone who gives a damn. They're going to carry you out in a short body bag," Darby gritted.

"You were always stubborn." Big 60 picked Darby up and threw her, crashing hard into broken chairs and desks.

Darby banged her head hard on the corner of a desk. Blood began to soak through her cap. She was dazed, but not unconscious. When she eventually got to her feet, Big 60 had his gun pointed at her.

"You think that scares me! Do it!" Darby showed no fear.

Bang!

Indigo had struggled with her nonthreatening injuries from the direct gunshots to her bulletproof vest to shoot Big 60 in the arm. It seemed to awaken the angry giant within. He heaved desks and chairs out of the path that led to Indigo.

Bang!

Darby had scrambled for her gun and put a bullet in the side of Big 60's head. There was a hard thud side from his body crashing to the floor. Darby thought she'd feel some sort of satisfaction, but her spirit still felt empty.

Liam finally found them. He rushed in and smothered Indigo with a desperately loving hug. She was in pain, but his gesture was soothing. Besides, she was relieved to know he was still alive. Liam saluted Darby, who then returned the exchange with a smile.

"There's one more we have to get. We can't let him escape." Darby went to exit from the classroom.

Liam blocked the door. "I know you wanted to be the person to pull the trigger, but someone else did the work for us." He led the way to the classroom that was across the hall. NYPD officers were moving in and out of the room.

Darby pushed her way through the mayhem of officers rejoicing in victory. Some were taking pictures and selfies with the dead man and the bloody mask. Detective Lawson was standing over the unmasked man, who had a single exit wound to his head. Darby didn't know what to expect. The plastic surgery had transformed his face, and he had put on a significant amount of muscle mass. Admittedly, she told herself that she would have never been able to recognize him on the streets. She still needed proof that it was Tyrus, so she didn't allow herself to experience any happiness.

Liam continued to hold tightly to Indigo's hand. "Can we pick up on that kiss again?" He fell to one knee.

"My friend. You have a lot to learn. This isn't a romantic place to propose to anyone," Darby tried schooling him.

Liam fell flat on his face and went into shock. Apparently, Whisper's wayward bullets had hit their mark. Blood was coming from his thigh and armpit. It didn't look like any major artery was punctured, but he'd lost a considerable amount of blood as he'd tried desperately to find Indigo.

"No! Not again." Indigo rushed to give him some help. Her body was shaking uncontrollably. She gently rested his head on her lap. "Please help him. Please!" Indigo hadn't heard the sound of her voice since she was sixteen. She spoke with a heavy Spanish accent.

CHAPTER 46: JUSTICE

News of the major takedown went viral in minutes. The mayor of New York stood alongside the chief of police as he gave his report to a prearranged press conference. Detective Lawson had requested that he'd wait until the lab came back with the results from the masked man's fingerprints, but she had no influence on the situation. Besides the pressure he was receiving from top officials, the chief knew his officers and those alike needed hope and to feel justice was served.

The press conference was held outside of the hospital where Lt. Marks, Liam, and wounded officers from the battle were being treated. It was late in the evening, so portable spotlights were used to add to the hospital lighting. The chief's opening remarks explained it was still an active investigation, so he wouldn't be at liberty to answer any questions after giving his statement.

"First, let's have a moment of silence for the brave men and women who honorably lost their lives earlier today," he began, and there was a moment's silence.

"They will be given respectful recognition later once all families have been notified of their deceased loved one.

"Working collaboratively with multiple task forces throughout the city, we were able to get the final suspects responsible for the officers' lives that were taken in what now has been called the Brooklyn Blitz. Additionally, we have sources that have confirmed the sniper, who was also responsible for the hit on Detective Ross and attempted murder of our Lieutenant Marks, was declared dead at the scene. Other key suspects believed to be the heads of an organized gun smuggling crew throughout several states were also declared dead at the scene.

"The NYPD and other government agencies will be working jointly to expedite the handling of the assailants who were arrested today. We are confident the evidence and statements gathered will prove vital to cases that are still pending throughout the United States and possibly abroad.

"Justice was served today for the great people of New York who we've sworn to serve and protect, and especially, for the men and women who proudly wear and have worn the uniform across this wonderful nation."

CHAPTER 47: UNFINISHED BUSINESS

An unmasked Tyrus moved freely about the city. His strategy was to be miles away from the attack at the abandoned school. The gunman, who'd stepped in for him, agreed to the risky mission because he was given ten thousand dollars upfront and promised another twenty once it was done. He didn't know he'd volunteered for a possible suicide mission. Big 60 was given strict orders if things went bad to put a bullet in his head and leave him to be found by the police.

Tyrus thought he had the perfect plan in place, but didn't think Darby would seek help from the NYPD. He mourned the loss of his true brother, Big 60, and for the first time, he felt completely alone. He still had unfinished business to take care of before disappearing for good.

He watched Aunty Cynthia turn off her bedroom light. He waited another fifteen minutes to make sure she was in for the night. Then he walked up to the front door. Tyrus took out the key he had gotten from Noah. "Baby brother, you continue to help from the grave," he thought with a smirk on his face.

Tyrus walked through the modest home and grew angrier and angrier. There were family photos on walls and shelves and even a recent picture of Rowan, but none of him. It was like he didn't exist. Fueled by rage, he stormed into Aunty Cynthia's bedroom with cruel intentions.

He flicked on her bedroom light and kicked the foot of her bed. "Wake up, old lady. The big bad wolf is home."

The body underneath the bedspread didn't stir. Tyrus grabbed a handful of the blanket and yanked it completely off the bed. "I said, wake up!" He was stunned to see Cord laying on the bed with a gun pointed at him.

Rip came from behind and removed Tyrus's gun from his front waistband and his cellphone from his pocket. She patted him down to make sure he wasn't concealing any other weapons. Cord slowly got up off the bed with his attention focused squarely on Tyrus.

"Take a seat." Rip was direct.

Tyrus moved towards the lone chair in the room. He attempted to sit.

"Not there!" Rip and Cord yelled in unison.

"Don't you see Mel is sitting there?" Cord said emphatically.

"That fool almost sat on me," Mel voiced.

Rip gestured for Tyrus to sit on the bed.

"I know he's crazy, but you are, too. I'll sit down, but don't forget y'all work for me." Tyrus was pissed. He couldn't believe he had to listen to two insignificant soldiers from his crew.

Smack!

Rip hit Tyrus sharply across his face. She wanted to make the point that they were in charge, not him. Tyrus peed a little in his underwear. It was at that point he realized his life was truly in danger. He was clearly taller and more muscular than the other two, but Rip had an imposing presence. He tried to appeal to their emotions.

"Big 60 was my brother!" Tyrus patted his chest hard. "Would still be alive if you two would've just followed directions. All hands on deck!"

He struck a nerve with Cord and Mel. They had spazzed a bit out of control. The man they considered a friend and who believed in them was dead. With his free hand, Cord pounded on the side of his head several times. Mel paced the floor like he was an airplane about to take off. He was mumbling something, but Cord couldn't make out what he was saying.

"We're … following … directions." Rip stared coldly at Tyrus. "He told us to protect the lady and the child from you."

Tyrus was stunned. He couldn't believe the man he called a brother and who went into battle against Chameleon, Darby, and her crew, was the same who seemed to have planned his imminent demise.

"I'll double what he's paid you," Tyrus tried to barter for his life. "Plus, put you two in command. Wait, your imaginary friend can be second in command."

"You can't buy loyalty. Let's go!" Rip demanded.

"Triple," Tyrus pleaded. "I have a duffel bag of money in the car. It's yours. And you have my word. I won't harm anyone. I'll disappear for good."

"Let's go or I'll put a bullet in your head right now." Rip was losing her patience.

141

Tyrus moved slowly as he was still calculating a way to save his life. With her free hand, Rip pointed at Aunty Cynthia's disheveled bed. Then she followed behind Tyrus as they exited the bedroom. Cord carefully remade the bed exactly like the photo they had taken earlier and fluffed the pillow that was on the chair where Mel sat.

Days earlier, Darby had arranged for her parents to take Rowan and Aunty Cynthia out of town for an impromptu family trip to Canada. They had left a day before the battle was supposed to kickoff. She needed to go into battle, knowing they were far away from harm. Aunty Cynthia couldn't resist a road trip with a little girl who brought life back into her broken spirit.

Thud!

Just as they reached Tyrus's car, Cord whacked him hard on the back of the head with a solid collapsible police baton. Tyrus was out on his feet. He crashed hard onto the hood of his car and awkwardly fell to the ground. His right leg twisted in a position that it wasn't physically designed to do.

CHAPTER 48: MONSTER

Darby was alone in the waiting room of the hospital. Except for some bruised ribs, a headache, and minor cuts on her hands and face, she was managing her injuries without taking any pain meds. She peered out of the window and thought of Rowan and her parents. It had been a few hours since the chief's press conference had ended. The sea of officers, reporters, and onlookers had all but gone. There were a few podcasters spying in the shadows waiting to get more juicy news.

She felt mentally drained, but knew tomorrow she would have to answer a relentless barrage of questions from her FBI superiors. Darby thought about calling her parents, but she didn't want to compromise their safety. Although there was a rush to identify the unmasked man suspected of being Tyrus, she had the intuition that he was still alive.

Tia and Liam were in the same intensive care unit of the hospital. Tia still had rotating uniformed NYPD officers guarding the outside of her room. She had regained consciousness and was able to breathe on her own. She communicated here and there by whispering a few words, but mostly she and Kate stared longingly at each other. The medicine Tia was on not only kept her pain to a minimum but also forced her to sleep on and off throughout the day. Kate managed to hide her guilty tears of feeling at fault for Tia's predicament by bawling her eyes out whenever Tia was sound asleep.

Though Liam had lost a lot of blood, doctors felt he would recover from his gunshot wounds. His athletic physique and the fact he had muscles stacked over more muscles played a major role in him surviving his injuries. There was just one thing his doctors needed, and that was for him to awake from passing out from the significant loss of blood.

Ting. Ting.

Indigo had set her smartphone's alarm to ring every hour. It was her reminder to check on Darby. She knew if Liam was still on his feet, he would continue to do everything in his power to protect Darby. So she made it her responsibility to protect them both. When she entered the waiting room, Kate was placing a hospital blanket over a sleeping Darby.

"How's Liam?" Kate whispered.

At first, Indigo searched her pocket for her pencil and pad, but then decided to speak. "He should pull through. But he's still unconscious. And Tia?"

"Soon she'll be back to her feisty self." Kate stared at Darby. "I got my monster from under the bed. I hope we got hers," she mumbled under her breath.

CHAPTER 49: FRIEND

Tyrus woke up with a canvas bag fastened tightly over his head. He couldn't see through it, but sensed that the room was well lit. His leg, that had bent awkwardly during his fall, felt like it was broken in two places. The pain sent shock waves to his brain. He tried desperately to free himself from the chair he was tied to, but had no such luck.

"Let me go! Do you know who I am?" Tyrus struggled violently in the chair. "Let … me … goooo!"

"Stop! Stop! Talking!" Cord yelled as he covered his ears. "Enough!"

Though Tyrus didn't know where they had taken him, he was confident Rip wasn't in the room with them. He knew she was the one calling the shots and despised him. She would've whacked him with something for yelling.

"Bro, I'm sorry. I was scared. I thought I was alone." Tyrus tried to appeal to Cord's unique sympathy. "You know about being alone. Right?"

Cord didn't respond. He paced the floor, but was careful not to get too close to Tyrus.

"Big 60 was my friend, too. He's gone. Maybe we could be friends. Marvin too." Tyrus was ready to say anything to be freed.

"His name is Mel," Cord said.

Tyrus felt he was getting closer to getting Cord to release him. "My bad. Ask Mel if he would like us to be friends."

Cord went silent again.

Tyrus pretended to give Cord some time to speak to Mel. The thirty seconds of quietness felt eerie to him. He wasn't sure if Rip had walked into the room, if the crazy dude was actually having a conversation with his imaginary friend, or there was a gun pointed at his head. Nevertheless, Tyrus knew he had to work fast before Rip showed up.

"Mel said he wanted to be friends, right?" Tyrus questioned.

145

Cord paced the floor again. "No, he wants me to shut you up forever."

Tyrus didn't say another word.

Rip was in another room watching them from a glassed window. She had already redialed a number three times, but it just kept saying FaceTime was unavailable. Each time she called, she was careful to flip the camera on her phone to face the wall.

"What's wrong with you? Answer the damn phone," Rip said in frustration.

CHAPTER 50: WITNESS

The rising sunlight danced on the bits of dust that floated inside the waiting room. Indigo and Kate talked throughout the early morning. They didn't pull straws or agree to see who would stay awake to keep watch. Though both were drowsy with sleep, they weren't going to let Darby out of their sight.

Kate's smartwatch was low on battery life but had just enough to flash a text alert that Tia was awake. She had arranged for the rotating officers to keep her up-to-date of Lt. Marks's activities.

"Tia is up. I'm going to make sure she's comfortable." Kate yawned as she spoke.

"I know how you can make her comfortable—brush your teeth." Indigo pinched her nose.

"Funny. I see you two have become friendly." Darby had finally opened her eyes and freed herself from the blanket. "Any word from the lab?"

"Well, good morning to you too," Kate responded. "Not yet, but I'll stay on them."

"Your phone had been vibrating throughout the early morning," Indigo told Darby.

"And who brought the talkative one?" Darby joked.

"Seriously, maybe your family was trying to reach you," Indigo insisted on being helpful.

Darby reached for her iPhone. It had been connected to the wall outlet that was just within reach from where she had curled up to sleep. She noticed several missed call notifications from a familiar number. It was Tyrus's burner phone number. Her suspicions were hauntingly accurate. Tyrus was still alive.

She looked up to tell the others about the missed calls, but Kate was screaming into her phone at a forensic lab tech, and Indigo had stepped out of the room. Darby retrieved her blue hat from the small table and stuffed it onto her head. Her thoughts were in a tug-of-war between calling back the number or waiting to be called again. Darby

147

saw that the last call came in over an hour ago. Curiosity had gotten the better of her so she went to redial the last call, but just before she did, a FaceTime call came through.

Darby answered the call. Her phone's Internet service was a bit choppy from the interference and dead spots caused by the structure of the hospital. The image she saw first was of a wall covered with peeling yellow paint. She could tell the caller was in some sort of car repair shop.

"Your job is to listen." Rip was in no mood to have a back-and-forth conversation with the person responsible for the death of her mentor and friend. If she wasn't following the wishes of her deceased friend, she would've already tracked Darby and her partners down and made quick work of them.

Darby was startled to hear a woman's voice. "Where is Tyrus and who is this?" she thought. Darby obeyed the strange woman's demand by remaining quiet.

Rip took Darby's silence as an agreement to her terms. "Big 60 wanted you to know he didn't know Noah would be killed. I know he was battling his own demons because of it."

Darby sighed hard. Hearing unapologetic excuses about the death of her true love fell on deaf ears. Darby closely observed the images she saw as the caller walked out of one room and into another. She increased the volume on her phone. Darby wanted to listen for any distinguishing voice patterns. She waited patiently for the caller to finish her leisurely stroll through what looked to be a large, abandoned automotive shop.

Soon Darby could see faintly in the distance what seemed to be someone bound to a chair. As the caller moved closer, she could see that the person tied to the chair had his head covered. Darby assessed the person fastened to the chair was a male because of the clothes the person was wearing.

Darby noticed a man quickly flash across the screen. She couldn't make out his face because the wiry man never looked back. The same strange man reappeared in view. He didn't waste any time removing the hood off the man who was tied to the chair.

Tyrus needed a few seconds for his eyes to adjust to the light that had just bum rushed his senses. He looked around the room. Cord was standing next to him with the canvas bag in his hand. Tyrus wasn't sure, but he had thought he saw someone moving by a stack of used tires. Then he spotted Rip pointing her phone at him. At first, he thought that was better than having a gun aimed at him, but he finally noticed the plastic that covered the floor underneath him and it caused his heart to race out of control. His face was full of fear and he wet his pants.

"Don't do this. I have money! Plenty of it!" Tyrus pleaded.

Darby recognized the voice, but not the face. Her ears told her the man begging for his life was Tyrus, but her eyes refused to believe it. The image of the man she had constructed in her brain was light years apart from whom she was seeing here for the first time.

"He could've walked right by me," Darby thought.

The caller continued to walk directly over to the guy who knew his time with the living was short-lived. Her pace never changed rhythm. The male figure was no longer in view.

"Please. Don't let them kill me," were Tyrus's last words.

Bang!

It was a single shot to his temple that ended Tyrus's reign. The caller shot while Darby watched from the waiting room of the hospital. Darby recognized a freshly done tattoo of the number 60 on the caller's shooting hand. Darby had just witnessed a murder but couldn't look away.

"You finally have a face to your shadow. Out of respect for our mutual acquaintance, we will not to harm you or your family. But that contract will be null and void if you pry into our business. He also told me to tell you to let the Boss family rest." Rip kept her camera pointed at Tyrus. "Don't come looking for his body. You won't find it."

Click!

Darby was speechless and somewhat shocked about what she just witnessed. She couldn't believe she had just watched Tyrus get murdered. But what had her stunned the most was the fact she didn't have any sadness for him. She was numb. Yet seeing him beg for his life gave her some unresolved vindication of Noah's killing.

Snap! Snap! Snap!

"Hello. Are you hearing me?" Kate tried getting her attention.

"Sorry. I was a little distracted. But it's done now." Darby came back to reality.

Kate babbled on. "Nothing's done. That's what I've been trying to tell you. The dead mask man is Maxwell Richmond. Not Tyrus Boss. The prints don't match!"

Indigo returned to the waiting room with three travel-sized toothbrushes and a tube of toothpaste. "I bring comfort."

"Oh, you still got jokes. I think I liked you better when you didn't speak," Kate chuckled. "By the way, the lab results came back. No match. Shit!"

Darby grabbed her phone charger from the wall outlet. "I was wrong. We got our man!"

Kate and Indigo looked confused.

"Since Noah's death, I had this eerie feeling in my gut, like he couldn't rest in heavenly peace until I killed the people who saw him take his last breath. I know it sounds crazy or hard to believe. But after what we did yesterday, he can rest now," Darby said without giving away much emotion.

"Are we really done?" Kate questioned.

"For now," Darby affirmed. "Our mission is done."

"What are you going to do?" Indigo questioned.

Darby took a deep breath and smiled. "FaceTime my parents, talk to my daughter until she gets tired of talking, which won't happen, and then get a new phone number. Too many strangers have this one."

"Cool. You say it's done, it's done." Kate knew Darby was hiding something, but Tia needed her more. "I have a girlfriend who needs me to play nurse."

"I'll go with you. I need to make things right," Indigo said with sincerity.

"Oh, the hell you will." Kate snatched the tube of toothpaste from Indigo. "Maybe one day you can make things right. But this isn't the year."

"Ha. Ha."

Kate and Indigo laughed as they gave each other a fist bump before going their separate ways.

CHAPTER 51: THE MEETING

Darby was about two months into her suspension from the Bureau. She was still getting her base salary until her upcoming board hearing. Her superiors had wanted the rogue agent gone from the agency once her debriefing was completed. They fought hard and called on favors within the Bureau and Federal Government, but her highly publicized role in taking down an arms trafficking ring, and a hit-man for hire whose body count of civilians and NYPD officers seemed to be growing daily, were her free get-out-of-trouble passes.

Rowan had been a great distraction for Darby during her suspension. The two of them were now joined at the hip. Darby smothered her little girl with love and attention from the moment she woke up in the mornings until the bedtime stories were read. The only breaks were when Rowan was in school. Time spent with her daughter had Darby feeling at peace with whatever the decision would be declared at her board hearing.

On the other hand, Darby's father was relentless in trying to convince his daughter to meet with Aunty Cynthia. Whenever it was time for a play-date between Rowan and Aunty Cynthia, Darby was quick to have another obligation she couldn't break. Darby was determined to resist the pressure put on by her father but it was the burden of knowing it was the right thing to do that kept her spirit prisoner in a straightjacket.

The itch she couldn't scratch had become too much to bear, so she agreed to take Rowan to her next visit to see Aunty Cynthia. Darby felt Rowan would be a great buffer between her and Aunty Cynthia.

"There's no way she'd try to hurt me in front of Rowan. Right?" Darby tried convincing herself.

Visiting day had finally come. Darby sat in the car outside Aunty Cynthia's house. As she worked up enough courage to exit her car, Rowan busied herself by unfastening her seatbelt.

"Mom, let's go! Second Grandma is waiting for us," Rowan said as she darted from the car.

Ring! Ring!

Rowan rang the doorbell and waited with great anticipation for her Second Grandma to come open the door.

"Shit!" Darby said.

"Is that my favorite grandchild?" Aunty Cynthia was giddy as she blindly swung open her screen door.

"Yes, Second Grandma." Rowan grinned hard. Then she quickly squeezed past Aunty Cynthia and ran into the house. Rowan was anxious to get to one of Aunty Cynthia's freshly baked chocolate chip marshmallow cookies.

Darby and Aunty Cynthia stood at the front door, staring at each other. It was like they were playing a game of Who Blinks First. Aunty Cynthia tried her best not to show that she was completely caught off guard. The tension between the two seemed like it was about to pop, so Darby was the first to look down at her own feet.

SMACK!

Now it was Darby who was caught off guard. In a matter of seconds, Aunty Cynthia had pulled Darby in with what appeared to be a loving hug but in an instant pushed her away and given her a smack across the face. Darby backed off the steps without a fuss.

SLAM!

Aunty Cynthia slammed the screen door and quickly shut her front door behind her. With her back leaned against it, she slid down until she was sitting on the floor.

"I'll have my parents pick her up!" Darby hollered from the walkway. Her face was still stinging from the unexpected smack.

"I'm not ready yet!" Aunty Cynthia yelled back. "But thank you for coming."

CHAPTER 52: PROTECTION

Rip and Cord watched the exchange between Aunty Cynthia and Darby. Cord had wondered why they were still keeping surveillance on the old lady that Big 60 had told them to protect from Tyrus. He thought their job was done once they had killed Tyrus.

Yet Rip finally had eyes on the person who had taken Big 60's life. She felt that her persistence and determination had paid off. Darby wasn't what she had dreamed her to be, but now the woman in her dreams had a distinct face.

"He said not to harm her," Cord reminded Rip of one of Big 60's last requests.

Rip didn't respond.

Instead, it was Mel who added his two cents. "I know why. She's pretty."

Rip never took her eyes off Darby. She watched her as she returned to her car. Rip engaged her ignition switch and waited for Darby to pull out of the driveway. She was ready to follow Darby until the ends of the earth.

BOOKS BY LAWAYNE WILLIAMS

REVENGE SERIES
Penalty Flag on Life Part I

STANDALONE TITLES
High School Diva
Rehabilitation